Praise for

Karen Eisenbrey's
A Quest for Hidden Things

"This tale is built on two very powerful things—great storytelling and beautiful prose. The author writes each scene with such rich detail it transports you into the action. It's a classic fantasy adventure with a touch of cozy. I loved the intrigue and the unexpected twists and turns. Highly recommend! Karen is a fabulous writer. *A Quest for Hidden Things* is my favorite read so far this year."

    -JL Henker, fantasy sci-fi author and host of the *Women Fantasy Authors* YouTube Channel

"*A Quest for Hidden Things* deftly interweaves multiple timelines and multiple points of view in a charming and magical coming-of-age tale. ... As Crane and Ketty grapple with their own magical abilities, blossoming romance, and the repercussions of generational trauma, they discover a greater mystery looms and with it a threat that could annihilate their villages and beyond."

    -M.K. Martin
author of the *Survivors' Club Chronicles*

"Because Karen Eisenbrey already developed this universe in her *Daughter of Magic* trilogy, reading this prequel series feels like coming home to a richly conceived world of magic, beauty, tenderness, and misconceptions overcome through grace. This is the universe I want to live in."

    -Benjamin Gorman
author of *The Convention of Fiends* series

Deep River Rising

Karen Eisenbrey

Published in the United States by
Not a Pipe Publishing Ink-Corporated L.L.C.,
www.NotAPipePublishing.com

Trade Paperback Edition

ISBN-13: 978-1-956892-75-8

Cover Art by Michaela Thorn
Cover Design by Benjamin Gorman
Map by Karen Eisenbrey and Steven E. Scribner

Dedication

This one's for all the teachers who help us imagine
something different from the way things always were.

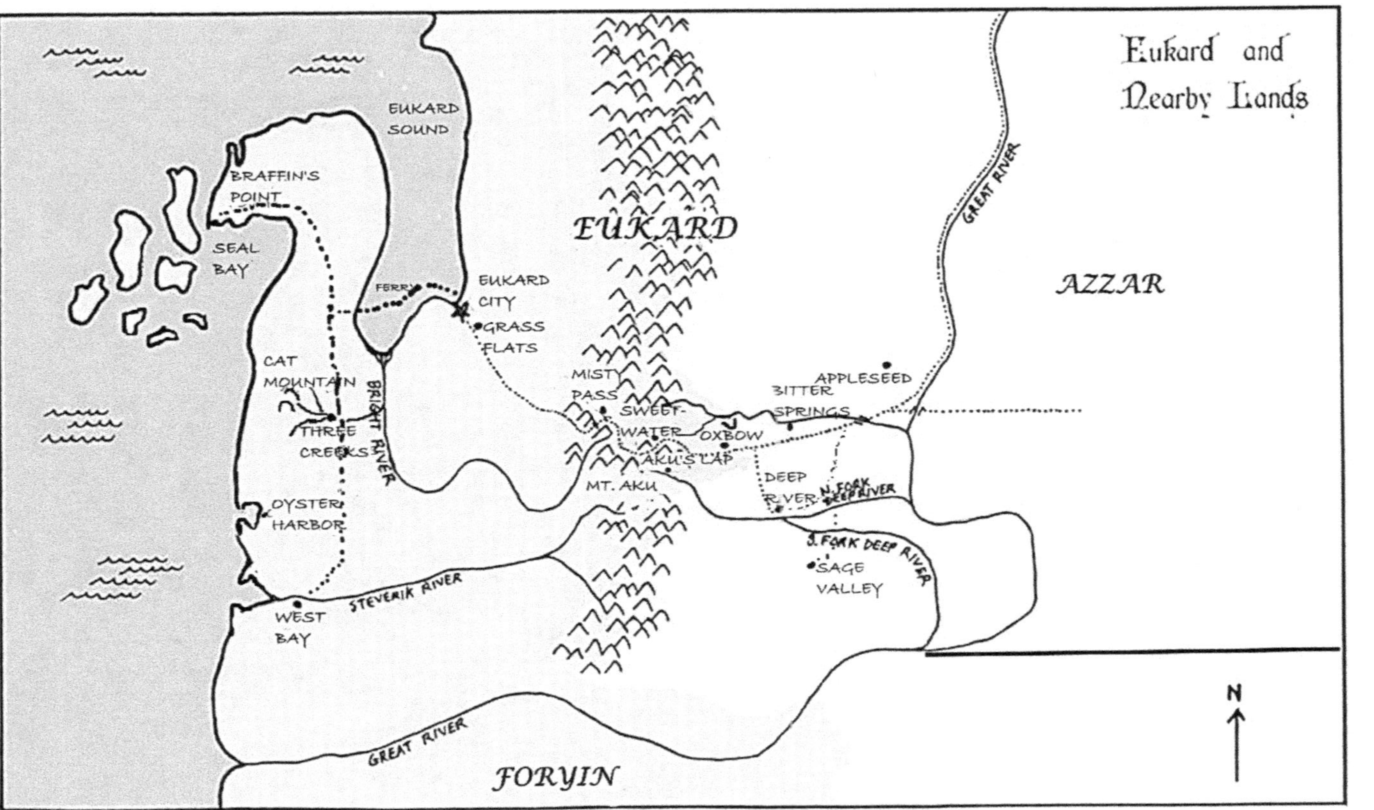

Eukard and Nearby Lands
EUKARD SOUND
BRAFFIN'S POINT
SEAL BAY
FERRY
EUKARD CITY
GRASS FLATS
EUKARD
AZZAR
GREAT RIVER
CAT MOUNTAIN
BRIGHT RIVER
THREE CREEKS
MISTY PASS
SWEET-WATER
OXBOW
AKU'S LAP
BITTER SPRINGS
APPLESEED
DEEP RIVER
N. FORK DEEP RIVER
MT. AKU
OYSTER HARBOR
S. FORK DEEP RIVER
SAGE VALLEY
STEVERIK RIVER
WEST BAY
GREAT RIVER
FORYIN
N

CHARACTERS

(In alphabetical order; major characters in **bold**)

Alill (uh-LIHL), daughter of brewer Lollum (age 11)

Alryg (AHL-rihg), son of potters Kryg and Alna (age 13)

Ati (AH-tee), wife of Yshna, stepmother of Sunnea (age 41)

Brak (brack), farmer, husband of Mynna, cousin of Breff (age 30)

Breff, farmer, son of Raffyn, husband of Tiek, father of Brettif and Tibreff (age 21)

Brettif (BREH-tif), son of Tiek and Breff, twin brother of Tibreff (age 0)

Briato (bree-AH-tow), weaver, husband of Keena, father of Tiek, Kiat, and Brynnit (age 39)

Brynnit (BRIH-niht), youngest daughter of Briato and Keena, sister of Kiat and Tiek (age 9)

Crane, wizard, child of Stell and Knot (age 18)

Elic (EH-lihk), teacher in Deep River, son of Sudi and Ohme, brother of Jagree, sweetheart of Sunnea (age 19)

Farl, miller in Deep River, husband of Lynka, father of Farlyn, Rynk and Foli (age 40)

Farlyn (FAHR-lihn), daughter of millers Farl and Lynka, sister of Rynk and Foli (age 13)

Foli (FOH-lee), son of millers Farl and Lynka, brother of Rynk and Farlyn (age 6)

Huvro (HOOV-roh), farmer, son of Hurik and Vari, brother of Rovhi (age 19)

Jagree (JAG-ree), apprentice blacksmith and stablekeeper, son of Sudi and Ohme, brother of Elic (age 11)

Jelf, Keeper of Records in Deep River, Stell's uncle (age 60)

Keena (KEE-nuh), wife of Briato, mother of Kiat, Tiek, and Brynnit (age 38)

Kiat (KEE-aht), daughter of Briato and Keena, twin

sister of Tiek, sister of Brynnit (age 19)

Knot (naht), wizard on Mount Aku, lover of Stell, father of Crane; formerly known as Yrae (age 38)

Lafa (LAH-fuh), son of farmers Ylaf and Lania, brother of Ylani (age 15)

Liko (LEE-koh), son of cobblers Tiko and Kolma (age 9)

Lynka (LIN-kuh), wife of Farl, mother of Farlyn, Rynk, and Foli (age 39)

Myn (old) (Mihn), mayor of Deep River, father of Mynna and Young Myn (age 50)

Myn (young) (Mihn), son of Old Myn, brother of Mynna (age 6)

Mynna (MIH-nuh), daughter of Old Myn, sister of Young Myn, wife of Brak (age 19)

Ohme (OH-mee), blacksmith, husband of Sudi, father of Elic and Jagree (age 41)

Raffyn (RAFF-ihn), retired farmer, father of Breff and Lynka (age 55)

Rovhi (ROH-vee), farmer, son of Hurik and Vari, brother of Huvro (age 23)

Rynk (rink), son of millers Farl and Lynka, brother of Farlyn and Foli (age 10)

Senri (SEHN-ree), son of Sinth and Liba, brother of Silib (age 6)

Silib (SIHL-ihb), daughter of Sinth and Liba, sister of Senri (age 10)

Soorhi (SUR-ee), past teacher in Deep River, uncle of Yrae (deceased)

Stell, innkeeper in Deep River, mother of Crane, lover of Knot (age 36)

Sudi (SOO-dee), midwife, Stell's best friend, wife of Ohme, mother of Elic and Jagree (age 40)

Sunnea (soo-NEE-uh), daughter of Yshna, Elic's sweetheart (age 18)

Tibreff (TEE-bref), son of Tiek and Breff, twin brother of Brettif (age 0)

Tiek (TEE-ehk), wife of Breff, mother of Tibreff and Brettif, sister of Kiat and Brynnit (age 18)

Tikum (TEE-kuhm), retired farmer, father of Tiko (age 60)

Walgyn (WAHL-gihn), traveling fiddler (age 20)

Ylani (ee-LAH-nee), daughter of Ylaf and Lania, sister of Lafa (age 9)

Yshna (EE-shna), tailor, father of Sunnea, husband of Ati (age 40)

Deep River Rising

Chapter I. Curse Lifted

Elic lay in bed, his eyes squeezed shut. He couldn't face another morning. This was the end.

If Yrae won't kill me, I'll do it myself. There's my razor. Or I'll leave Deep River. I did it before. I'll ...

Elic's eyes snapped open. He stared at the ceiling, almost afraid to move. His dusty, dim-lit room was the same, but something had changed. Elic sprang from bed and almost fell in his haste.

"It's just like the time when we escaped!" He caught his breath. That was twice he had thought or spoken freely of the curse that had weighed on him all his life. Heavier each day, though, since his return from accompanying his best friend Crane on the first leg of his quest to break it. Elic had gone along to make sure Crane made a good start and didn't give up without trying. That was the most Elic could do; he wasn't a wizard. When he was sure Crane would see it through, Elic returned to Deep River, where the curse was waiting for him. Yrae's Curse oppressed and isolated everyone in the village, but they didn't know it. Only Elic knew and suffered because he had escaped.

Even the fleeting thought of ending his own life was a sign. It could mean only one thing. Crane had done it. Yrae's Curse was broken.

Since returning three months ago, Elic found his work as the village teacher was the only thing worth getting up for. The only thing anyone could have relied on him to do. Even mustering the energy to do that had grown more difficult with each passing day. It had become a monumental struggle to rise from bed and make the short walk to the one-room schoolhouse. Thinking of the children kept him struggling against his burden of despair and helplessness. Only with them was he anything like himself. He had spent his time outside of school alone in his house with the shutters closed. He hadn't bothered to light a lamp. He had only started lighting a fire when the weather grew too cold to bear. He appreciated the hot meals his mother brought. Without them, he might have forgotten to eat, but he didn't cook for himself. Too much effort.

Now Elic moved with renewed energy and purpose. He lit a lamp and kindled a fire in the fireplace. He washed his face, and carefully shaved, the razor's grimmer application forgotten. Something glinted in the lamplight. Elic stared at his reflection, at the gold ring in his left earlobe — the betrothal ring, a sign of promises made before he sank into the pit. After a moment, he finished shaving. He dressed quickly, growing more eager for the day.

"I need to sweep." He threw open the shutters over the east window. On the sill, an agate the size of a hen's egg glowed a rich amber in the filtered light of the gray morning. This was Elic's most prized childhood possession, yet he hadn't even glanced at it in months. He picked up the stone, cold and smooth in his hand, and recalled the summer day when he was eleven, hunting agates in the dry riverbed with his friends and bringing home the biggest one any of them had ever seen. He rubbed it against his shirt to remove the dust. "I need to dust the whole place." He opened another set of shutters and strode across the room. "Then I need to build a wall here, so we can have two rooms, like a proper house." He opened shutters at the front of the house. "And add more rooms."

Outside, a magpie's harsh voice croaked, "Ek!" like it was saying Elic's name. He looked out the front window as a cloaked figure stepped onto the porch. He yanked the door open. Crane stood at the door, his fist raised to knock. In his other hand, he held a wooden staff almost as tall as he was. They stared at each other. Elic's voice caught in his throat. Without a word, he grasped Crane's hand and dropped to his knees, pressing the hand to his forehead.

"What are you doing?" Crane asked. "I don't need one

of your jokes right now."

Elic looked up at him. His best friend was annoyed, but for once, Elic meant no mischief. He felt something closer to fear. "I'm sorry. I never met a powerful wizard before. How should I act?"

Crane pulled Elic to his feet. "You haven't met one yet." He smiled crookedly, and tears glinted in his eyes. "But it's good to see your face again. I ... I dreamed you were in trouble."

"I was. That's over now." Elic whooped and pulled Crane into a warm embrace. "Welcome home. I was afraid we'd never see you again. I thought ... Well, never mind." He stepped back, holding Crane at arm's length to study him. "In that old cloak, you look like a real wanderer. And the staff suits you now. You're a greater wizard than I knew."

Crane was taller and darker than anyone else in Deep River. Nothing new there, but something was different about Crane's familiar face. He was younger than Elic, not even eighteen. No, he was eighteen today, though his sparse, stubbly beard made him look older. That, and the look in his eyes.

Crane frowned. "I didn't do anything."

"But you must have defeated your enemy," Elic insisted.

"I defeated no one. Perhaps he never was my enemy. I served him, and brought him here, so he could make a fool of me."

"I'm sorry to hear that, even if it doesn't make any sense." They'd sort it out later. "But you're home, safe and sound, and that's what matters. I heard you were ill."

Crane nodded. "I heard the same about you. Sunnea came to see me."

"Yes, she told me." Sunnea was his sweetheart; his betrothed now. But she never talked to Crane if she could help it. It must have been difficult for her to make the visit. Crane was staying at the Blue Heron, his mother's inn. For reasons Elic didn't understand, it wasn't considered proper for girls or women to go there. For Elic's sake, she had crossed into forbidden territory to speak to someone she feared. Much as he appreciated that she had reached out to Crane in his place, it bothered him that she had been forced into that position when she wasn't even his wife yet.

Elic shook off the unpleasant feelings. "Did you enjoy the apples?"

"They were good medicine." Crane smiled, which changed his whole face. For someone who usually looked serious, he had a surprisingly warm smile. It cheered Elic to see it again. "Thank you for sending them. But I hoped to see you."

"I wanted to come, but ... it's hard to explain. Maybe I expected too much of you."

"I expected too much of myself." Crane sank into his favorite porch chair, and Elic sat next to him in the other one. Crane reached out and flicked Elic's earring. "So, are you still planning a spring wedding?"

"I guess. If she wants to."

"What do you mean, *if*?"

Elic opened his mouth to speak, then closed it again, unsure how to voice what was on his mind. He stared out over the road, empty at this hour, and tried again. "I thought of releasing her from our agreement." He was ashamed to admit how much he had let Sunnea down over the past months. He had spent almost the whole time since their betrothal hiding, oppressed by the curse he couldn't talk about. And they had made their promise under that curse.

"Why? She loves you. She's been trying to help you."

"I'm beginning to see how much." Elic got up and paced. "Things have changed. I'm not the person I was."

"You're not the only one who's changed. Does she want to break with you?"

"I don't think so. But she's so innocent, and fragile."

Crane shook his head vehemently. "That's nonsense! She's strong and brave."

"So she's your friend now?" Elic asked.

"She is," Crane said. "It's up to you to make her my sister. Set the date. You'll see."

Elic smiled. Maybe the idea of parting from Sunnea was only a symptom of an illness that hadn't quite passed. "When the apple tree's in blossom." He gazed at the bare branches.

"That's so far off," Crane said. "I'll be sorry to miss it."

"Why? Where will you be?"

"I don't know." Crane peered off down the road as if seeing a million horizons beyond. "But I can't stay here."

"You just got back. You were going to be our wizard."

"Don't you think Deep River has suffered enough wizardry? You're better off without it. Without me." Crane's face knit into the familiar scowl.

Elic had missed that grouchy face without knowing it, though the reason Crane wore it now eluded him. "Crane, why are you so unhappy, on this day of all days?"

Elic gasped. "You don't know?"

"Don't know what?"

"The curse — it's gone!"

Crane stared as if he couldn't believe what he'd heard. He stepped down from Elic's porch into the frosted grass below and gazed up at the sky. "It's gone." A sunray beamed through a gap in the clouds, lighting his dark face. "He wasn't lying."

Elic didn't know who Crane was talking about, but he didn't ask. He stood on the porch, in the unusual position of being taller than his friend.

Crane closed his eyes and spread his arms, his face still alight with sunbeam and smile. He murmured something Elic couldn't quite hear and vanished in a flash of white feathers. Elic watched in amazement as a large white bird circled overhead, then flew away toward the west. He blinked. Crane couldn't be gone. He'd just come back. He'd lifted Yrae's Curse and freed Deep River. How could he leave now?

Elic sank down on the step and stared at the spot where his friend had stood a moment before. Only the prints of his boots remained, etched in frost. Crane was gone, and with him, Elic's elation. He'd awakened with a sense of freedom and possibility. Now it all drained away, leaving him empty.

Chapter 2. Old Promises

Elic and Crane had grown up as close as brothers. Their mothers were lifelong friends. Crane didn't have a brother of his own, or a father for that matter. Elic had been Crane's protector when they were children. Crane had always been different, in looks and temperament, even before he discovered his magical power. Elic had compelled the other boys to include Crane even if they didn't like him. He couldn't do anything about the girls. They regarded Crane with suspicion; even fear. Especially after he revealed his uncanny abilities. Why would anyone dislike or fear Crane? He'd never harmed anyone but himself. In spite of an intimidating frown, he had the kindest heart of anyone Elic knew.

Crane didn't need a protector now. If he could break Yrae's Curse and change his own form, he could do anything. He had the power now, and Elic had ... nothing.

Something soft bumped his hand. He looked down at Embers, a young tortoiseshell cat that liked to hunt around the school. A mouse dangled from her jaws.

"Prrt?" Her prey muffled her voice.

"No, thank you. I don't need it." Elic scratched the cat behind her ears. She had often tried to supplement his diet with rodent offerings. If she ever had kittens, they would be well fed.

At the sound of footsteps, the cat bounded away. Elic looked up, filled with wild hope. Was Crane coming back?

No, Crane was a great wizard now. A great wizard wouldn't come back to a place like this.

Elic's heart fluttered as he watched Sunnea approach. He fingered his earring. Crane had encouraged him to set a wedding date, as if he knew more about it than Elic did. Elic had felt something for Sunnea for as long as he could remember, a boy's blind devotion. But how could he trust his heart? It had chosen her under a curse that stifled curiosity. What kind of choice was that? She deserved better.

Sunnea looked as pretty as ever. Her short blue cloak brought out the blue of her eyes. The fur lining her hood matched the gray of her woolen dress. Under the hood, a few strands of golden hair caught the morning light.

Elic smiled and held out his hand. "Good morning."

She squeezed his fingers. "Elic, your hand is freezing!

How long have you been sitting here with no coat?"

"I don't know. You're out early."

"I've been up for hours! I woke up with a feeling of such possibility. I saw an eagle."

"It was a crane," Elic corrected her. He had no doubt that was what Crane had become, though Sunnea couldn't be expected to recognize a bird she'd never seen before.

She frowned. "I know what I saw."

Elic dropped her hand. It wasn't like Sunnea to argue or even express a strong opinion.

"You came to tell me that?"

Her returning smile died on her lips. "Who ... who else would I tell? I wanted to see if you were better. Because something feels, I don't know. Different. Better."

"It's the curse. Crane broke it."

Sunnea beamed. She had more reason than most to be happy about this news, having seen Elic at his worst under its weight.

"I wasn't the only one out early," she said. "I met Stell and your mother, talking in the middle of the road. Stell said Crane's gone."

Stell was Crane's mother. She would feel his absence even more than Elic did. He nodded to show he'd heard and tried again to smile.

"But you're back with us," Sunnea said. "I was afraid for you, but Crane said you'd be yourself again soon."

"I hope I am. Have I missed anything important?" He didn't want to think about Crane right now.

"I don't know." She sat beside him on the step. "Did I tell you Mynna married Brak?"

"You might have. When?"

"About a month ago."

Elic didn't really care about this news. He knew Mynna, a woman about their age. He'd never liked her. She was Mayor Myn's daughter and had a haughty attitude. Brak was a farmer about ten years older and not a part of Elic's circle. He could think of nothing more to say on the subject. Talking about marriage with Sunnea, even someone else's, set Elic on edge. In spite of Crane's encouragement, he didn't trust his own curse-tainted decisions enough to set a wedding date with Sunnea. Not that there was anyone else he wanted to marry. Maybe he should live alone.

They sat together, not quite touching, though some of Sunnea's warmth reached Elic. She smelled like summer. The cold morning brightened. The frost melted and Crane's footprints disappeared with it. To Elic's eyes, that patch of grass would never be the same.

Sunnea cleared her throat. "Mother told me to ask you again about the betrothal supper. Could you come the day after tomorrow?"

Mother was Sunnea's stepmother, Ati. Elic didn't remember Sunnea's birth mother, who had died when they were young children. Ati had been trying to have Elic to supper since the betrothal three months before. It was part of the tradition and should have taken place already. Until today, he hadn't felt up to such an event. He knew the meal would be good — Ati was an excellent cook — but he needed all his strength to endure her prickly personality.

"Day after tomorrow," he repeated.

They sat in silence.

"He's the second friend to leave you behind," Sunnea said at last.

Elic shook himself. "What do you mean? Who is?"

"First Soorhi, now Crane. They go where you can't follow."

He hadn't considered that, and it bothered him that she had. But she had always been attentive to detail, whether in nature, schoolwork, stitchery, or relationships. When they were children, she usually found more agates than anyone else. In fact, she had spotted Elic's prize, though he had put in the effort to dig it out of the riverbank. When he had offered to share it, she had laughed and said she would have it one day.

She was right about Soorhi and Crane, though they had gone in different ways. Crane had flown on wings of magic; more than a year ago, the old teacher Soorhi had died — simpler, but more mysterious. It seemed almost disrespectful to refer to an institution like Soorhi as a friend. Mentor, yes. Example. Model. Elic missed him and guessed he always would.

"Speaking of Soorhi," Sunnea continued, "Stell is writing down all her stories, and she remembered Soorhi had notes of tales he collected somewhere. If you can find them, she'd like to see them again."

"I'll look around."

"I have to get back now." Sunnea rose. Elic felt the chill of the morning as she left his side. "You should go inside. You're freezing!" She squeezed his hand and kissed him, her lips a warm circle on his cold cheek.

It was how they always parted — a squeeze of the hand, a kiss on the cheek. No more, no less. Now it was too much. Or not enough.

Chapter 3. The School

Sunnea's summer scent lingered. Like flowers. Roses. But how, when nothing bloomed? He remembered years ago when he'd watched his mother making soap, she had done something with flower petals to make part of the soap smell good. Elic always washed with plain soap. Sunnea must use soap infused with flowers, with roses. If they married, their home would always smell like summer.

Elic's little house was warm by the time he went back inside. This had been Soorhi's house from the time he started the school until his death. Before that it had belonged to Elic's grandfather, Greelin, who built it. He had skillfully mortared together hundreds of river rocks into four stout walls. He'd used wood only for floor, doors, and roof framing. Trees were scarce, but rocks were everywhere. He had included a second door in the west wall of his one-room house. Elic had never seen the point of it. He dimly remembered a family story about it being intended as the entrance to walled or fenced garden that was never built.

For the first time in months, Elic had an appetite. Although he hadn't prepared a meal for himself in a long time, he had some food stores: root vegetables and a basket of apples in the cellar; onions hanging from the rafters; a hunk of cheese, a slab of bacon, and most of a hard sausage on the coldest windowsill. Dried apples, too, thanks to his mother's efforts. A sack of dried beans, another of porridge oats, but no time to cook either for breakfast. Most of a meat pie Sunnea had given him the day before ... or the day before that? He had eaten only a small portion without really tasting it, to be nice. Sunnea had made it because she remembered how much he had enjoyed the dish the first time she shared it with him, soon after they were officially courting in the spring. There was enough left to make a good lunch or two. He found half a loaf of bread his mother had brought over a few days ago. It was stale, but toasted, it went well with sliced cheese and sausage.

Elic sat down with this meal and thought about Stell's request. Tales Soorhi had collected? Collected when? Soorhi wasn't from Deep River originally. He had come to the village and started the school more than thirty years before, when he was already well along in life. He had spoken of his dream that someday, someone in Deep River would need to know how to read. Every student had heard the story. Elic liked Soorhi's poetic way of saying he wanted to share the gift of schooling with a town that lacked it.

But he'd had another life before Deep River. A life that must have included collecting tales. Where would those be? Not in the school. Elic or the children would have found them by now if that was where they were. Most likely they were in the house. When Soorhi died, Elic had inherited the job, the students, the house, and whatever bits and pieces Soorhi had acquired in his long life. At the time, grief and the daunting new responsibility had left Elic too overwhelmed for the task of going through the old man's things. They still waited in a crate under the bed.

He pulled it out. There were a lot of loose papers inside. The notes Stell wanted were probably among them. On top was a stack of ink and charcoal drawings, all of water birds. They showed considerable skill. He'd never seen Soorhi sketch anything so detailed and wondered who the artist was. The drawings were organized by type of bird. That much was in character for Soorhi. One group was all cranes. Elic recognized them from the picture Crane had in his room, which Soorhi had given to him longer ago than Elic could remember. There were also herons, familiar from the painted sign at the inn; and ducks, swimming and flying. Elic had never seen a swimming duck. There was not enough water anywhere near Deep River for any of these birds. Maybe there had been once, when the river still ran. Before Yrae's Curse.

Under the drawings was another stack of pages. The paper was yellow and brittle with age, the writing faded but legible. A quick scan told Elic these were the notes Stell had asked for. He lifted the stack carefully. Something dropped from the middle of the pile and thudded back into the crate. A small, thick book. Elic set the notes on the table and picked it up. It had been made with care of durable materials, but it was not the work of a trained bookbinder. The thick, soft pages were irregular, stitched into a binding of worn, greasy felt.

Elic flipped through a few pages and recognized Soorhi's large, uneven handwriting, an inky fingerprint at the beginning of each line. The entries were dated — the book was a diary. These pages contained brief accounts of the weather and mundane activities. Elic turned to a random page farther along that included a more detailed entry.

> *My Crane' is gone'. I don't think we' will meet again, no matter what he' promises. A great wizard wouldn't come' back to a place' like' this.*

Elic slammed the book shut, his heart thudding. Soorhi had written Elic's own thought! How was that possible? The entry was dated over thirty years ago. Fingers shaking, he opened the book to a later entry, dated about six years in the past.

> *Stell's boy has finally re'veale'd his gift. I wish he' could have' chose'n a le'ss dramatic way. It's a good*

thing I have 'eye's in the' back of my he'ad,' as Ordy use'd to say. As soon as I had my back turne'd, all the' boys crowde'd around Crane'. I saw his hand in flame's. I didn't think, I move'd: ove'r my de'sk and to his side', whe're' I smothe're'd the' flame's with my hands. I don't know why I wasn't burne'd. He' was badly injure'd. He' has le'arne'd a hard le'sson, but now he' knows what he' is. It still strike's me' that Ste'll name'd him what she' did. He' re'minds me' so much of my poor little' fellow. I wish I could se'e' his face'.

Elic remembered that day. At twelve, Crane seemed to think he had everything to prove and had terrified his classmates with his magical accident. Elic blamed himself for it. He had been thirteen then, confident and respected, a leader of boys. He had dared his friend to sneak into Jelf's library and read from the spell books reputed to be there. He hadn't expected anything to happen, unlike Soorhi, who seemed to know what was coming. Even before this incident, Crane had been Soorhi's favorite.

The diary entry raised more questions than it answered. Who was his *poor little fellow*? Who was Ordy? What did he mean, "I wish I could see his face," when he'd known Crane since birth? And how could he see the flames with his back turned? It was like talking to someone you've known all your life and discovering you don't know him at all.

A loud knock interrupted Elic's musings. "Elic, are

you in there?" He went to the door and opened it. His eleven-year-old brother Jagree stood on the porch. "What's the matter with you? We're all waiting."

"I'm sorry," Elic said. "I lost track of time. It's been quite a morning." Elic dropped the diary on his bed and pulled on his coat. "I'm ready. Let's go."

Together, they walked to the schoolhouse nearby. It was larger than the house but of similar construction.

"Did you see that big white bird early this morning?" Jagree asked. "It was huge! I never saw anything like it. I wonder why it flew west, not south."

"I saw it. I think it's the last we'll see of that one." To change the subject, Elic added, "Are you taller than you were yesterday?"

"Maybe. Mam says I eat enough for two."

Shouting and laughter carried through the door even before Elic opened it. Usually, he was in the schoolroom well ahead of the morning class and could easily keep these older boys in order. There were only four of them this year, ranging in age from ten to fifteen. Left on their own this morning, they had started a noisy game.

Elic stepped into the room with a loud, "Good morning!"

The boys froze where they were, two of them standing on desks. A ball dropped to the floor and rolled to Jagree's feet. He picked it up and handed it to Elic, who put it into his pocket and walked to the front of the room. He tried to look stern, but it was difficult. His students had kept him sane the past few months.

When Elic took over the school, it had never occurred to him to change anything. Maybe under Yrae's Curse, he didn't have a choice. Soorhi's pattern worked well enough, though. Children usually started at age six or seven, though some were ready younger, and others started later. They received basic instruction in reading, writing, and figures. As they were ready for it, they also studied Deep River history and the natural world. Just as there was no prescribed age for entering school, there was none for leaving. It was common to leave school at fourteen or fifteen. Some left earlier, while others stayed on. Boys and girls were separated at age ten, before they could distract each other too much, but received the same instruction.

When not in school, the boys in the morning class were either apprenticed to local tradesmen or helped work their family's farms. They looked typical of Deep River people. They had either some shade of brown hair, like Elic and Jagree, or blond, like Sunnea. Most had light skin that tended to freckle. None were particularly tall. None looked like Crane, with his black hair, dark skin, and towering height. None had a spark of magic. Crane didn't resemble anyone in Deep River, not even his own mother. Elic had never considered who he did look like, though now it seemed obvious: he must resemble his father. Whoever that was.

"Boys, this is a special day, and not only because I lost track of time and came late to school," he said. "Time for a little Deep River history. How many of you have heard of Yrae's Curse?" Jagree was the only one to raise his hand. "That's not surprising," Elic continued. "You younger ones might not have felt it. For some reason, it didn't affect children, but it would have touched you eventually. Lafa, how did you feel when you woke up this morning?"

Lafa was the oldest in the class, a farm boy of fifteen, and good-looking enough, girls noticed his brown curls and blue-green eyes. He wasn't the best student, but he was strong and good-natured. He furrowed his brow. "Taller. And I wondered where the road went, and what's past the mountains." He blushed and looked down. "That's silly, I know."

"It isn't silly at all," Elic said. "Yrae's Curse kept you from wondering those things. Now the curse has been broken. You never knew you were trapped, but now you're free."

"If this is Deep River history, how come you never told us before?" ten-year-old Rynk asked.

"I *couldn't* tell you. I wanted to, but I couldn't."

"Who stopped you?" Alryg asked. He was thirteen.

"Yrae did. Or rather, his curse did."

"Yrae, the Mad Wizard?" Alryg's brow furrowed. "What does he care about us?"

"I wish I knew," Elic said. "All I know is, longer ago than I can remember, something happened to this town. No new people came here, even to pass through, and no one living here considered leaving. It was difficult for anyone past childhood to wonder about things, or plan to do anything a new way. As soon as anyone noticed things weren't right, the thought would slip away. It was almost impossible to talk about it. Crane believed the spell had something to do with him. And he's the one who finally broke it."

Caught up in the story, the boys cheered. As they settled down again, Lafa asked, "How do you know all this?"

"Soorhi told me some," Elic explained. "He must

have had a better grip on his thoughts than most. Last summer, I went part way with Crane on his trip. We discovered the edge of the curse's range. When I stepped out of it, I knew freedom for the first time. That's how I felt this morning."

It was a wonderful feeling, the freedom to tell his students these things, and to talk of Crane as the hero he should have been all along. He had been scorned for his appearance and feared for his power, but he had saved Deep River. And now he was gone, on a new adventure where Elic couldn't follow. But he could tell the story.

The afternoon class was larger with ten students, mostly younger children who wouldn't have felt the curse. There were a few older girls who might have. Kiat certainly had. She was nineteen, the same age as Elic, and had technically graduated three years ago. She visited school occasionally to help with the younger children, something she had started when her younger sister was new to the class. Rynk's older sister Farlyn, at thirteen, might have begun to feel it, too. He wasn't sure about Alill or Silib. Alill was eleven and Silib only ten, but sometimes children that age surprised him with their maturity. He repeated his lesson for the whole class. None of the students knew of the curse, though they had all heard of Yrae.

"I thought Yrae was just someone in stories," Kiat said. "You say he's real?"

"I hope not!" Alill cried. "Whenever I hear one of those stories, I get nightmares."

"Crane believed he was real," Elic replied. And yet, what had Crane said? *He never was my enemy. I served him, and brought him here.* That couldn't be right.

Perhaps Elic had misheard. "It's possible the stories are exaggerated."

"Why is he called 'The Mad Wizard', then?" Silib's younger brother, Senri, asked.

"He was supposed to be cruel and unpredictable," Elic said. "But the curse on Deep River didn't actually hurt anyone. It only kept us from thinking about certain things."

"What does Yrae look like?" Ylani asked. She was Lafa's sister, only nine, but already a more diligent student than her brother.

Young Myn, the mayor's son, jumped in before Elic could answer. "He's got claws instead of fingernails, and fangs dripping blood! His eyes are on fire! And —"

"I forgot to ask Crane that," Elic interrupted. He frowned at the little boy. At six, he had a colorful imagination, but it wouldn't do to let him terrify the other children. As it was, Ylani's eyes could hardly go any wider. "I don't think you have to worry about meeting him."

In the first row, the little girl next to Ylani raised her hand. She wore long brown braids and a serious expression.

"Yes, Brynnit?" Elic asked. She was Kiat's baby sister, though not a baby anymore at eight. No, nine now. She was a quiet girl who listened more than she spoke. Her questions were usually to the point.

"Why is the river dry? Is that the curse, too?"

"The river is dry because it was dammed," Elic replied.

Ylani whispered something to Brynnit, and they both giggled into their hands. Elic was relieved Ylani no longer looked frightened, but he couldn't overlook the disruption.

"What's so funny?" he asked.

"Teacher, you said a swear," Ylani replied, struggling to control her laughter. "About the river."

"I did?" When he got it, he chuckled himself. "Sorry, I meant the river was blocked by a dam, not that it was damned."

"Isn't that the same as cursed, though?" Brynnit asked.

"I don't know if the river being blocked is part of the curse or not. We'll have to wait and see if the water returns."

Liko, at nine the oldest of the boys in the class, gazed out the window while the younger boys called out questions. Some of them were silly, just what Elic knew to expect from six-year-olds, but it was plain all of the students were excited and curious about what had happened.

Once they got past Yrae, they were especially full of questions about what lay beyond Deep River. Elic was scarcely qualified to tell them. In his life, the farthest he'd been from home was a day's walk, but he shared what he knew. He rooted around in a drawer and found an old map of Eukard that must have been Soorhi's. Although it was tattered and faded, Elic doubted much could have changed in his lifetime. He spread it out for the children to look at. It showed rivers, mountains, towns, and cities. Together, they found Deep River. Close by were several locations with vaguely familiar names: Bitter Springs, Sage Valley, Stony Creek, Oxbow.

"What are they?" Liko asked. This activity had finally

captured his attention.

"They're other villages," Elic replied.

Brynnit frowned and stared hard at the map. Then she brightened and gazed at Elic with a sparkle of excitement in her eyes. "You mean, with people in them? Other people, like us?"

"Yes, exactly." It was a new idea to him, too. Had he ever thought about other people? "Look here." Elic pointed to another spot on the map, across the mountains from Deep River. "That's Eukard City, the capital of Eukard." He didn't know anything more about the capital. He couldn't remember when he'd ever spoken of it with anyone, but Soorhi must have mentioned it.

"What's a city?"

"What's Eukard?"

Elic did his best to answer their questions, though he found it as difficult as they did to imagine a large city or to understand how all the places on the map were part of one bigger place. Soorhi must have told him some of this, because he was able to answer most of their questions, or at least begin to answer them. For all of them, it was their first glimpse of a wider world.

Chapter 4. Questions

After school, Elic went home and collected Soorhi's notes for Stell. On the way to the inn, he stopped at the Village Hall, where he had often interrupted Crane in his studies of magic. He hoped to catch the Keeper, Jelf, before he left for the day. The old man was still at work in his library, just off the large main room. The shelves held the village register of births, marriages, and deaths, logs of daily events, a few old storybooks that must have arrived with the founders, and those mysterious spellbooks.

The old Keeper started when he looked up and saw Elic in the doorway. "It's been a while since you dropped by. Is it true, then? Yrae's Curse ..."

"... is broken, yes."

Jelf nodded. "Today felt different. I hear Crane is gone again."

Elic sighed. "On feathered wings."

"Too bad. Winter would be a good time to have a wizard on hand to work our weather. He told me he was learning that skill." Jelf shrugged. "And I'll miss the boy just for himself. I wanted to put something in the log, but I've struggled with it all day." He squinted at the page, then dipped his pen and wrote quickly. "There. What do you think?" He turned the book so Elic could read the entry.

Weather: cold, overcast, heavy frost. Curse lifted. Crane gone. A new day.

"That's all?" Elic asked.

"It's enough. So, what can I do for you?"

"I have questions about Soorhi, and you knew him best."

"Which wasn't very well. He had a way of keeping himself hidden. But go ahead and ask."

"Did you know he kept a diary?" Elic asked. "I found it this morning."

"I never saw his diary, but he mentioned it once, toward the end of his life. He wanted me to have it for the library, after you'd had a chance to go through it. He was frustrated because he couldn't find it and he was afraid it might have been burned."

"I found it jumbled in with a lot of papers and things. I meant to sort them, but I never did, until today."

"Yrae's Curse," Jelf said, and Elic nodded. How long would it be before they stopped noticing every new thought? "What did you want to know?"

"He mentions people I've never heard of — Ordy, and someone he called his 'poor little fellow.' Do you know who they were?"

Jelf shook his head. "Sorry, I don't. He must have known lots of people before he came here."

Before he came here. So Soorhi did have a life that had nothing to do with anyone in Deep River. Elic didn't know why he hadn't thought about it before today. Was that Yrae's Curse, too?

Elic headed for the door, pausing when he remembered one more question. "Jelf, do you happen to know whether Crane brought someone with him when he came home?"

Jelf grinned. "I think you should ask your brother about that."

Not the answer Elic expected, but his parents' house was across the road from the inn. He could make another stop. In a way, he was glad to pay several visits. He had barely left his house since returning from his adventure with Crane. Then, it had been high summer. Now, winter was at hand. The air smelled like snow, though Elic wasn't sure he could trust his nose. Was it cold enough? The sky had remained the same flat gray since morning, and the sun had not appeared again after lighting Crane's departure. It set now with little show, bleak daylight slowly fading to dusk.

Under Yrae's Curse, Deep River had been Elic's whole world. He hadn't known or imagined other places. After he escaped the curse and returned, Deep River had become a prison, his personal pit of despair. With the veil of the curse ripped away, he could see the village in the dying light as it truly was: a pathetic little cluster of houses on the bank of a dead river, in no way important to the rest of Eukard. There was no reason to believe any outsider would want to visit, curse or no curse.

Elic found his brother cleaning up in their father's forge. The boy was an apprentice blacksmith and already showed great skill for his age. Pap trusted him to return every tool to its proper place at the end of the day, even unsupervised.

"Jagree, you were at the inn a lot while Crane was home," Elic said. "Did he bring anyone with him?"

Jagree blushed and looked past Elic with a dreamy smile. "I thought everyone knew. He brought a girl — a healer — named Ketty. She had the most beautiful red hair." Jagree sighed. "She's gone now, too."

What was this about a girl? She must be something to affect Jagree this way. Maybe that was good news for Crane, but it didn't fit at all with what he'd said about bringing his enemy to Deep River.

"Are you sure there wasn't someone else? A man? Maybe a wizard?"

"There was that man we —" Jagree broke off, eyes wide. "No. No one else. Sorry."

"It's all right, Jagree. You can tell me. The man you ...?"

"I promised! I promised Ketty and Stell I wouldn't tell anyone."

"It might be important," Elic said. "The secret is safe with me."

Jagree glanced around, then moved closer to Elic.

"Crane didn't bring him to the inn," he whispered. "Ketty found him, way out in the pine woods. I thought he was dead."

"Who was he?"

Jagree shrugged. "I don't know. We brought him back here, and Auntie Stell put him to bed in her room."

"What did he look like?"

"I don't know, like an old man," Jagree said. "Not *old* old, but Pap's age or so. And ... foreign."

"Foreign, how?"

"Like not from around here," Jagree said. "Darker than Crane, with a big beard and wild, bushy hair."

Before Elic could ask more questions, the door opened. "Jagree, supper's ready," Mam called. "Elic! It's good to see you out of your house. Did Sunnea find you this morning?"

"Yes."

Mam smiled, asking no more about the uncomfortable visit. "That's good. She's been worried about you. Stay for supper?"

"Thanks, I'd love to." How could he turn down a home-cooked meal? He'd take the notes to Stell later.

Chapter 5. Evening at the Blue Heron

The sky had grown dark by the time Elic left his parents' house. His breath steamed in the cold. The town was quiet; he was the only one out. He hurried across the road to the Blue Heron. As soon as he opened the door, the inn embraced him in light, warmth, and friendly clamor. Almost every seat was filled. Any man not at home was here. The crowd kept Stell in constant motion, serving supper and drinks. She never appeared hurried or lost her smile.

She was only a few years younger than Elic's mother but appeared more girlish than matronly. Perhaps it was her small stature, or her hair that she wore loose in the evening. The honey-blond waves swung and caught the lamplight as she moved. Even young men found her appealing, and the older ones adored her. She was on friendly terms with every man in town, but Elic's mother was her only woman friend. The other women avoided the inn and disapproved of Stell. Elic had never considered why this might be. Was it because their men were fond of her? Or was it yet another manifestation of Yrae's Curse?

"Evening, Auntie Stell," he called above the din.

She gave a delighted squawk and set down the plates she carried so she could hug him. "Here's my long-lost boy! It's good to see you, Elic."

He laughed at the enthusiastic welcome. He shouldn't have been surprised. Stell was like a second mother to him. "It's nice to be missed, and better to be back."

She released him. "If only you'd come while Crane was here."

"I know. But I saw him this morning." In his mind, he could still see the majestic white bird. Did she know about that?

"I'm glad. He was sullen when he left here. I hope you cheered him up."

"He was happier when he left me, though all I did was point out the obvious. He didn't know what he'd done."

She beamed. "Isn't it wonderful that he broke the enchantment?"

"Don't you mean *curse*?"

Stell shook her head. "I don't call it that. It didn't harm anyone, after all."

What about me? Elic wanted to ask. But no, the curse hadn't caused his trouble, so much as his escape and return. It hadn't hurt or killed anyone else, at least not directly. "Didn't it hurt your business, though? With no travelers passing through …"

"Maybe it did. How can I know? Maybe strangers would have brought more harm. If Yrae had wanted to hurt Deep River, we wouldn't be here now, talking about it." She smiled, a faraway look in her eyes. "But haven't you noticed? The enchantment always lifted if the need was great enough. So I don't think he wanted to hurt us."

Now that she had pointed it out, the truth was obvious. Lost travelers found their way to the inn, merchants arrived bearing material or medicine that couldn't be produced in Deep River. And every spring, the tax gatherer appeared without fail. Perhaps Yrae had a sense of humor.

"I see what you mean," Elic said. "We're still better off without it."

"I agree," Stell said. "I prefer to take my chances with the rest of the world, strangers and all. To think I tried to talk Crane out of trying to break it!"

Elic chuckled. "No one will be able to tell him anything now that he's a mighty wizard. Here, I heard you wanted these." He handed over Soorhi's notes without mentioning the messenger. He didn't trust himself to even speak Sunnea's name without giving away all his mixed-up feelings about her visit to the inn. About the promises they had made under Yrae's Curse.

Their bond, once so simple and sweet, had become tangled and confusing. "Be careful how you handle them. The paper is brittle."

"I'll put them in my room for safekeeping."

Her room. Was the stranger in there? Elic peered past her, but the door was closed, and he couldn't think of a polite way to ask. She slipped in and out quickly, revealing nothing.

"Will you stay for supper?" Stell asked when she returned.

"No, I ate at Mam's."

"At least have a mug of ale to celebrate, then. Deep River is free!"

He accepted the drink gladly and stayed a while to hear the talk. The tone was unusually spirited, even for the Blue Heron.

"I can't explain it," the weaver Briato said. He was Tiek, Kiat, and Brynnit's father. "I feel younger than I have in twenty years!" A broad grin creased his face.

"That's how I feel, too," said Breff, a farmer a little older than Elic. He was married to Tiek. They raised horses at their place a short distance from town. "Ever since I woke up this morning, I've wanted to run and jump like a colt. Like this!" With a shout, he sprang onto the table. Dishes rattled and ale slopped from mugs.

"You, too?" asked Kryg, Alryg's father. "I've been noticing all kinds of things I never saw before." He climbed up to join Breff, and several laughing guests pulled their suppers and drinks to safety. The two men linked arms and danced on the table. Somebody tootled on a little flute, and several others burst into song.

Elic was startled at first by this display. These men

could be boisterous in their talk, but he'd never seen anything to compare to this. Still, he remembered how he'd felt when he stepped beyond the curse's reach with Crane, and again this morning, when it was lifted. At least, how he felt after he got past the idea of taking his own life — that sense of freedom and possibility. Even if it made them giddy, he was glad grown men could share that feeling.

"I don't like it," grumbled Old Myn, mayor of Deep River for as long as Elic could remember. He was the only one not laughing or singing.

"Aw, you don't like anything!" the miller Farl teased over the din.

Stell patted Myn's shoulder and replaced his empty mug with a full one. He gave her a grudging smile but frowned again when Briato grabbed her hands and spun her around. They both whooped with laughter.

"Stop!"

The songs and laughter abruptly ceased. Elic recognized the voice — Yshna, Sunnea's father — but not the angry tone. The tailor pushed forward and glared at Briato.

"Take your hands off her! She's *mine*!"

Briato let go of Stell's hands and faced Yshna. "I recall she turned you down. Besides, she would have been mine once Stoli let her."

"Oh?" Yshna moved closer to Briato, who shrank back from the smaller man. "Did she have your baby?"

"Of course not!" Briato exclaimed.

All the men in the room now stared at Stell. Yshna shoved Briato aside and faced her. "Which one was it?" He waved toward the assembled men.

Her face paled, but she drew herself up and returned his gaze steadily. "No one here."

"Who was he, then?" Yshna took a step toward her. "Who stole you from us?"

Stell backed away from him. Before she could answer, Elic stepped between them and faced Yshna. "That's enough! Stell is her own person, not a thimble or a length of cloth. How old are you, twelve? Yshna, Briato, have you forgotten you have wives and families?" He couldn't believe he was using his teacher voice on men his father's age, but if they insisted on acting like children ...

The two men blinked and exchanged a sheepish look. "I ... I think I did forget, for a moment," Briato said. He smoothed his hair and sank back into his seat.

"Like it was twenty years ago," Yshna added. "Stell, please forgive me."

She still looked alarmed, though the color was returning to her cheeks. She stared at Yshna for a moment, then nodded and gave him a little smile. Elic stayed near her. He'd never witnessed an outburst like that before. They all loved Stell, but they didn't fight over her. He was sure no one had ever asked about Crane's father before. Even he hadn't, and Crane was his dearest friend.

"I don't like it," Old Myn muttered again. Elic agreed with him this time, but no one else paid him any attention. They were all staring at Briato and Yshna.

"Something has changed," Sinth, the carpenter, said. He hadn't been dancing or fighting, but he had joined the singing with as much enthusiasm as anyone. His brow furrowed as he searched the faces around him.

"Yes, it has," Elic agreed, happy to change the subject. He started to teach the same lesson he'd given the children. He got a few nods of understanding, but more puzzled frowns.

"Thank you, Elic," Stell broke in. "These fellows have been out of school awhile." Most chuckled in agreement. Back in control, she walked through the crowd and took her seat in the rocking chair by the fire. "Elic isn't wrong, though, that our village has been under a spell but now we are free of it. Let me tell you a story."

The guests near her turned their chairs, while those farther away drew up seats to face her. She always ended the evening with a story, or several, something her regular customers looked forward to. Tonight, the anticipation seemed higher than usual.

"Many years ago," she began, "the wizard Yrae — before he *was* Yrae — visited a village called Deep River. He made a mistake he couldn't bear for anyone to know about. So he conjured an enchantment to hide what he'd done."

"What did he do?" Briato interrupted.

Stell smiled at him. "That's the mystery, isn't it? It wouldn't be a story without a mystery."

"But why would he care who knew?"

"He was afraid," she replied without a moment's thought. "I imagine."

She sounded certain in her guess, even with the qualifier. But Yrae, afraid?

"Of what? Of us?" Breff asked, voicing Elic's thought. Most of the listeners joined his incredulous laughter.

"Ashamed, then," Stell amended. "Perhaps he had a reputation to protect. Or a family."

The idea that Yrae the Mad Wizard might have had a family silenced the crowd. Stell continued her story, in which the wizard hid from the world and invented an evil persona to repel the curious, all the time keeping a careful eye on Deep River. Her story, more compelling than Elic's lecture, held everyone's attention. She could not have known all those details about Yrae's motives, but invention was her gift, and the audience expected it. If anything, it made the story ring truer.

"... and so the young wizard, Crane, sought Yrae and discovered how to break the enchantment," she concluded. "He returned to his home only long enough to free the people. Then he set out on his next adventure, walking west."

"Flying," Elic corrected her.

"What?"

"He flew away. He is a great wizard now — he can take other forms."

"He flew away," she whispered, and smiled to herself. In a normal tone, she added, "The end."

The story cleared the tension in the room and calmed the rowdiness, while restoring a genial mood. Upon its conclusion, the guests engaged in quiet conversation about Yrae's Curse, over a last round of ale. Soon, it was as if these men had always known about it. And in a way, they had, feeling the curse's effects while it prevented conscious thought. They also spoke warmly of its breaker. Stell glowed with pride, and so did Elic. Crane was getting his due at last. If only he had stayed long enough to hear it.

Elic remained at the inn until everyone else had gone home. He helped Stell collect empty mugs as the last guests departed.

"It's late, Elic," she said. "You should go home."

"I will. I didn't want to leave you alone with that crowd, after Yshna's outburst. Their mood is mellow now, but ..."

"That was strange, wasn't it? Thank you for stepping in. I'm not sure I've ever seen them so wild. Not even when they were your age." She paused, a thoughtful look on her face. "Do you think it was because of the enchantment?"

He overlooked her choice of words this time. "I'm sure of it."

She sat in her rocker and pushed the hair back from her face. She looked tired, now that the other guests were gone. "I knew about the spell, but I never thought about it."

"You *couldn't* think about it. None of us could, except maybe Crane. And Soorhi. He told me some about it."

"It seemed harmless."

"Crane said he could see it — a net of magic over the village."

"A net? One we were all caught in. But it should have been a blanket."

"What do you mean?"

"N ... nothing. Only, wouldn't it have been better if the spell were like a thick blanket, protecting us from harm?"

She wasn't making any sense. Then again, her only child had just left her for the second time, and friends had treated her badly. He could excuse a little nonsense.

"It's too late for talk like this. Good night, Auntie Stell. Let me know if anyone gives you more trouble."

Chapter 6. Soorhi's Diary

Elic wasn't ready to sleep when he returned home, though it was late. Being among people all day had energized him. He still missed Crane, but as if he had been gone a long time — weeks or months instead of one day. Crane had done everything he could for Deep River. What more could Elic ask of him, other than to return someday?

Back at his own house, Elic lit the lamp. There was Soorhi's diary, right where he'd left it. He picked it up again and opened it to the first page. It contained a dated inscription in an unfamiliar hand.

> *Soorhi,*
> *I made' this book for you, so you'd have' a place' to write' your thoughts after you leave'. I didn't know I'd have' to give' it to you so soon. Think of me' sometime's.*
> *Clover*

Elic read the date again. Clover, whoever that was, had given the diary to Soorhi close to seventy-five years ago. It was in remarkably good condition for its age, but Elic resolved to treat it more gently. He carefully turned the page to Soorhi's first entry. His handwriting here was small and neat, unlike what Elic had seen before, though still recognizable.

> *I'm not sure' why Clover gave' me' this. Doe's she' believe' I'll forget her? I wish I could. I gue'ss I will write' down my life' story, such as it is, until I think of something better.*

He guessed? That didn't sound like Soorhi at all. He never *guessed* anything — he *knew*.

> *My name' is Soorhi and I'm fifteen years old. Ye'sterday, I left Apple'se'ed, where' I lived for the' past six years. I liked being settled, but maybe' I'm*

re'stle'ss like' Pop. It's time' to move' on and have'
an adve'nture'.

Soorhi's age explained the uncertainty, but *adventure* was not a word Elic had ever associated with Soorhi. Nor *restless*. The Soorhi he remembered was a disciplined, methodical old man. Everything had its place, and if an object was out of place, the whole school heard about it. He seemed to know everything, including subjects he could not have learned in Deep River. Elic thought again of the notes Stell now had. They must have been already old when Soorhi came to Deep River. Elic read on.

The're' are' diffe're'nt kinds of pe'ople' in the' world,
but I don't know what I am. I'm not a farme'r,
I'm not a town pe'rson, and I don't suppose' I'm a
swamp pe'rson anymore'. I wonde'r if I'll e've'r
know.

Elic was only on the first entry, and already the diary raised two questions for every answer. Soorhi, a swamp person? Elic had heard of swamp people, though he'd never met any. They were characters in stories, described either as roving bands of thieves, or as harmless migrant workers who kept to themselves. Illiterate, invisible, always on the move. He couldn't connect either image with the dignified old teacher, though Soorhi had been a very private person. Elic knew nothing about Soorhi's family. He'd never once spoken of them, and Elic hadn't thought to ask. He turned the page to the next entry.

I can't remember my mother's face, unless I close my eyes. Then, there she is. She looks tired. I lost my family when I was nine years old. Or they lost me. They were picking fruit outside Appleseed. Ersi was still a baby, so Mom took him along, but I had to stay and guard the camp. What did we own worth guarding? I never asked, but Pop would have said, "Our freedom." I think to him, it meant nobody knew where we were. I got bored one day and walked to town. I saw Clover teaching school. I didn't know her name at the time, and I didn't know what school was. I saw other children who looked happy. She invited me to join the class. I thought her very plain, with her pale eyebrows and lashes, and her hair pulled back tight, and I couldn't understand why the other children paid her such rapt attention.

That was the start of my troubles. I loved school, so I sneaked to town every day until Pop said it was time to leave. I tried to persuade him to stay, maybe move into town. He came with me to meet Clover, but instead of staying the winter in Appleseed, he left me there. Schooling had "ruined"

> *me', he' said. He' wouldn't e've'n le't me' say good-bye'*
> *to Mom and Ersi. So that's how 'I came' to live'*
> *with Clove'r and he'r brothe'r and the'ir mothe'r, who*
> *was too sick by the'n to take' care' of anyone'. Clove'r*
> *taught me' e've'rything she' could. Maybe' that's why*
> *'I love'd he'r.*

Elic sat up with a start. Had he read that right? Soorhi ... in love? That was more alien to his character than an adventure. Elic tried to picture the white-haired little man wooing a young woman. No, that wasn't right. Soorhi was a child when he met Clover. Perhaps he loved her like a mother or sister. The words in the diary, written when Soorhi was fifteen, implied something more; if not true love, an infatuation. He was the same age then as Lafa; not much older than Alryg or Jagree. A boy much like Elic had been not so long ago, dreaming of Sunnea.

Sunnea. He couldn't remember when he hadn't loved her. He had been making her little gifts, carrying things for her, writing notes, at least since he was eight years old, and probably longer. He took a lot of teasing about it at first, but he was the best fighter in his age group and soon put a stop to it. When she finally got her courtship ring, he was there to declare his intentions before anyone else had a chance. They had courted for a few months, and then he proposed marriage. It was a formality. She had been planning their domestic life for years, and the whole village had been expecting it almost as long. All that remained was the wedding itself.

Elic had hoped to be married right away. Sunnea wanted to wait until spring. She would be nineteen then, and the apple tree in blossom. A spring wedding, spoken of in summer, had seemed a lifetime away. Now, though ... Did he love her out of habit? Had she accepted him because Yrae's Curse wouldn't let her imagine another possibility? There was a whole world outside Deep River, of which Elic had seen only a glimpse. Could he live his life with only one adventure?

He had no answers, and wasn't sleepy yet. He adjusted the lamp and continued reading.

> Clover taught me everything she could. Maybe that's why I loved her. She's not even pretty. But she never loved me, except as a brother. Foo on that! She's going to marry Jod the orchardist instead of waiting for me, so I'm leaving. I can take care of myself now.

The entry ended there. The next one was dated two days later.

> I don't know why I said Clover isn't pretty. She isn't, but she's beautiful when she smiles at me. And she gave me what she could. If I'd stayed with Mom and Pop, I wouldn't have learned to read or write. Swamp people don't trust school. I asked Clover once what school was for, and I'll always remember her answer: "You learn to write so you

can put down what you're thinking and not keep it inside you. That way, you won't forget, and someone else can benefit, even if you're not there to tell them. So that's reading: understanding what someone else wrote so they wouldn't forget. Or to tell a story, or the best time to plant out new apple trees, or something that happened long ago. And that's history, so we can understand how things got to be the way they are. You learn figures so you can count things, or add them up, or figure how much you owe the man helping pick your apples." That might not be exactly what she said, but it's close. I thought of Pop when she talked about the man picking apples, and probably she did, too. He couldn't read or write, but I bet he could figure, because nobody could cheat him. But what good was reading and writing to someone like him? She said they might give him something interesting to think about while he works, or he might learn to imagine doing something different. I liked that word, imagine.

Elic did, too. Even Yrae's Curse couldn't interfere with the natural imagination of children. It was especially satisfying for Elic as a teacher to watch that imagination blossom when they received new information. Or when a curse was lifted. Who knew what new things they might imagine doing now? And it wasn't only the children, though Elic wasn't ready yet to examine his own future. He continued reading.

> *After that, Clover taught me some history of where swamp people might have come from, a long time ago when Eukard lost their last king and formed a new kind of government. There were people who didn't trust any form of government, so in protest, they left the settled parts of Eukard and scattered out. (That sounds like Pop — he could always avoid the tax gatherer.) There's no more written record of them, but maybe that's where I come from. Even Pop couldn't have given me that. I must thank Clover for it. I'll try not to be angry anymore.*

Elic sat back and rubbed his eyes. They were tired, even if the rest of him wasn't. They wouldn't stay open to finish this entry, the longest he'd seen so far. Had Soorhi been tired after writing it? It explained a lot, and nothing. Elic had assumed he knew all he needed to about the mentor he admired. The old teacher had given Elic, and Deep River, so much while keeping his own life hidden. Who was Soorhi, really?

It was late. Elic closed the diary and set oats to soak for the morning. He got into bed and blew out the lamp. He fell asleep almost as soon as he closed his eyes, only to open them again what felt like a moment later.

The room was light. Was it morning? No, only lamplight. But he had blown out the lamp. A familiar figure sat at the table, a short, slight old man with thinning white hair, who looked like he belonged there. He squinted at Elic.

"Soorhi!" Elic cried. "You came back."

"I left something here," the old man said. "Ah, here it is!" He picked up the diary.

"I read some of it."

"That's all right. It won't answer your questions." He rose and walked to the side door.

Elic followed him. "Won't you stay awhile? The children would love to see you, and there are things I never got to ask. You can have the house back if you want. I can —"

"I told you I can't stay here." It wasn't Soorhi at all, but Crane. Elic snatched at his friend's cloak to stop him. The fabric flowed through his fingers like water. "You are free," Crane said, and disappeared. Elic clutched the door handle and followed him. Outside, no bare apple tree or vegetable patch, but a pine forest on a summer morning. Elic was alone. He knew he had to return to Deep River, but he couldn't bear stepping under the curse again, alone.

"Crane!" Elic cried as he woke. He was in his bed. The room was dark. He got up and stumbled to the table. His hand found the diary, already familiar to his fingers. The dream-Soorhi was probably right — it wouldn't answer his questions. So far, it had only raised more.

Although it seemed he had slept only a moment, he

felt rested. When he checked the east, the sky was beginning to lighten. There was no point in going back to bed. He lit the lamp and built up the banked fire to cook his porridge and heat water for washing. While he waited, Elic opened the diary again and continued the entry where he'd stopped the previous night.

I'll try not to be angry anymore. I think I knew Clover was going to marry Jod before she told me. She wouldn't even go walking with him while her mother was alive, but when she didn't have to care for the old woman anymore, she started seeing him. I hadn't told her how I felt, so maybe it's my fault — how could she wait for me when she didn't know? Maybe if I went back now and told her ... No, No, NO!!! Because before she told me, I saw them together, in a kind of dream, only I was awake. And I heard Clover say, "Boys, I'm going to marry Jod." And two days later, she told us in exactly those words. I told her I'd be moving on. She tried to get me to stay, but I don't think she was surprised. Maybe she was a little sorry. I hope so. I'll never love anyone else.

Elic knew the feeling. Did he still feel that way? For so long, he had looked forward to the home and family he and Sunnea would build together. He couldn't imagine it with anyone else, but he had never tried. The kettle boiled, and he closed the diary. He washed his face and finished making breakfast, chopping up an apple to add to the porridge. He had almost forgotten the pleasure of a hot breakfast on a cold morning.

He didn't know what to make of the vision Soorhi described, if that's what it was. It sounded like some kind of magic, though not a kind Elic was familiar with. Crane's magic had never come so easily, unbidden. Not at that age. He'd had little knowledge of his own abilities, let alone the future. And Soorhi had never made a show of having any magical power. But one of the first diary entries Elic had read spoke of *eyes in the back of his head*. Soorhi had seen Crane's accident even with his back turned and extinguished the flames without being injured himself. Maybe the old man did have a touch of magic in him.

Though curious, Elic resisted reading further. It was almost time to open the school. He could excuse himself for being late once, on the day the curse was broken. Not on the day after. If he did it twice, the boys would never let him forget.

Chapter 7. Mysteries

Before Elic left the house, the side door caught his attention. In his dream, it had led to another place and time. Was there something special about it? Something magical? No, it was an ordinary door. Wasn't it? He gave the handle an experimental tug. The door didn't budge, and he chuckled at how easily he had floated through in his dream. He pulled harder. It moved but didn't open. He would have to go out and push from the other side.

It was a bright, clear morning. Elic crunched through the frosty grass to the side door. He leaned his shoulder into it and shoved. He sweated and puffed with effort until it groaned in protest and popped open. He stumbled inside, then turned and looked out from this new doorway at his vegetable garden and apple tree. A fresh view of a familiar scene.

Beyond the bare tree, the rising sun lit the Mountain with a rosy glow. The gleaming summit was marred by a dark smudge Elic had never seen before. He remembered Soorhi saying the Mountain — he called it Aku — was a volcano. Now the rumors of an eruption made sense. Some villagers thought they'd heard or felt it, the night Crane arrived home. It didn't appear to have had much effect, other than to give Aku a dirty face.

On a clear day, the snow-capped peak looked close by, but Elic knew it was many days' journey to the west. Crane had planned to follow the river to the Mountain when he set out to find Yrae. Elic wished he had asked Crane for the whole story of that venture, in which he had played such a small part. Now it was too late. He closed the stubborn door again and went to the school.

Elic was settled at his desk when the boys entered, laughing and shouting. The noise continued as they took their seats. Although they had no ball this time, they behaved more boisterously than the day before.

"Settle down," Elic said. "You're in school now."

"But Elic," Jagree protested, "we're free!"

Elic was in no mood to hear Crane's dream message from an eleven-year-old. "In this room, you call me *Teacher*. And you are free of Yrae's Curse. You are not free of me."

Jagree frowned but didn't argue. The shouting subsided with a few grumbles, and Elic began the first lesson of the day. He followed Soorhi's pattern, both in the order of lessons and in how he treated his students. He could be firm, even harsh, with some of them. Jagree was tough and could take it, along with most of the older children and a surprising number of the little ones. Others required a gentler touch. The last thing Elic wanted was tears in the classroom.

Teaching was hard work, much harder than he would have guessed before he took on the job. Although smaller, this class was especially challenging. The students were learning trades and could leave school at any time. Elic wanted them to stay as long as they could, though he couldn't say why. What did they get out of it? What had Soorhi written about imagination? That schooling could help a person imagine something different from what they had always known. Maybe that was it. So he worked hard to keep the lessons engaging, maintaining discipline even when he wanted to laugh at his students' antics. It had looked easy when Soorhi did it, and he was an old man. How had he kept it up all those years?

Elic had been at it only a year, and at nineteen, wasn't much older than his most advanced students. He had to work twice as hard to win and keep their respect. But he loved the work, and the children — the little ones running over with energy and wonder, and the older ones, poised on the brink of adulthood. He suspected they taught him as much as he taught them.

To Elic's knowledge, Soorhi had no children of his own. He'd been well suited to working with them, with a bottomless well of patience, and a deep delight in knowledge and learning. For some reason, he had seen a need in Deep River. He had started a school where there hadn't been one before. He settled in a town where he had neither roots nor family ties as if he meant to stay his whole life, even before the curse kept him there. Elic imagined what it might be like to leave Deep River, travel to another village, found a school as Soorhi had. It startled him that he could imagine it, and so easily.

At the end of the day, Elic went to his parents' house for supper again, to make up for the months he'd spent holed up by himself. Jagree was at the washbasin by the front door, scrubbing his hands. He grinned at Elic as he straightened up to dry them.

"So this is going to be a regular thing?" he asked. "Supper at our house?"

"Mam's a better cook than I am." Elic reached for the door handle.

Jagree held him back. "Not so fast. Now I get to tell you what to do: if I have to wash, you have to wash."

"But I haven't been working in a forge," Elic objected. "Or a stable."

Jagree crossed his arms and blocked the way. "Wash."

"Fine, I give up." Elic washed. They went in together and sat at the table.

"The inn's busy tonight," Jagree announced. He'd been helping Stell with the heavy work and stabling chores since Crane's departure in the summer. He liked to share any news he picked up.

"It was busy last night, too," Elic said.

"This is different." Jagree paused, obviously relishing the suspense. "Guests."

"What do you mean, guests?" Pap asked. "Stell always has plenty of guests."

"Not supper guests. Inn guests. Overnight guests."

They all stared, and Jagree smiled around the table.

Elic didn't know what to say. This was another sign the curse was broken. He wasn't sure why they'd want to, but people could come to Deep River again, and they wouldn't know why they'd never done it before.

"One of them is a traveling merchant, and there were some musicians on their way to someplace east of here; I don't remember the name," Jagree continued. "They're going to stay overnight for the market tomorrow. The merchant rode a big bay gelding and led a pack mule, and the musicians had two spotted ponies pulling a cart." Elic smiled to himself — Jagree would bring it around to horses. "The third fellow rode down from Oxbow on a pretty sorrel mare. He brought Stell something."

"Brought her what?" Mam asked.

"I don't know. Where's Oxbow?"

"North of here, an hour's ride or two," Mam said. "It's a good-sized town. There was a coach stop there in the old days."

"A coach? Like a wagon?" Jagree asked.

Mam laughed, but Elic wanted to hear about it, too. He and his brother had lived under the curse all their lives, and there were so many ordinary things they'd never experienced. At eleven, Jagree was young enough, he probably hadn't felt the effect of the curse himself. The adults around him had. Mam and Pap were remembering things they hadn't thought of in years, but Jagree had never known them at all.

"It's a way to travel," Mam explained. "You pay money to ride in a carriage that travels a regular route.

They change horses frequently, so they can travel fast and not stop for long in any one place."

At the mention of horses, Jagree's interest grew. "How many horses? Where does it go?"

"I don't know how many. Probably four or more. The westbound coach travels to the city."

Jagree nodded. He was probably still entranced by the idea of four or more horses. He frowned. "The city?"

Mam looked at Elic with a teasing smile. "Don't you teach him anything?"

"It never came up. She means Eukard City," he added, for Jagree's benefit, "but I don't know much more about it than you do." The morning class of older boys hadn't even studied the map yet. Elic decided to post it on the wall the next morning, so anyone could look at it. There wasn't much knowledge he could add.

"Talk to Jelf," Mam suggested. "He should have logs going back to the founders."

"That's a good idea," Elic said. "But what do Jelf's logs have to do with Eukard City?"

"Where do you think the founders came from?" She smiled. "When I was a girl, I planned to move there someday, but I married your father instead."

"And we're all glad you did," Pap said. "Is there any more stew?"

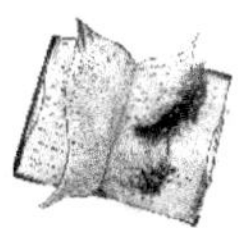

Elic mulled all this new information on his walk home. He'd expected change, but not at this fast a pace. Visitors had arrived. How long would it be before someone left? Someone besides Crane?

He drew water from the well and carried it inside to be ready for morning. He used a little of it to make tea before he sat down with Soorhi's diary. Already, reading it had become a habit.

> I've been thinking about my brother Ersi all day. I don't know why. I never forgot him, but I never thought about him much, either. I remember him as a tiny baby. I wonder what he looks like now. I'm about sixteen, so he'd be almost seven. He had brown hair, same as me, and dark blue eyes like nobody I ever saw. Like the sky at twilight. If I saw him again, I'd probably know him by that alone. Will he have to work hard in fields and orchards, like Pop? Or will he end up tramping around alone, like me? I don't suppose he'll get to go to school.

Elic couldn't get over the idea that Soorhi had a brother. He had never mentioned him, but Soorhi never talked about his past. Had the brothers ever met again after Soorhi left his family? Unlikely. Elic couldn't imagine not knowing his brother. Jagree could be a pest sometimes, less so as he got older. He was almost twelve — not really a child anymore. He had his own interests and talents. He was growing into a person Elic could talk to. It was difficult to be his teacher in the morning and his brother the rest of the day. Elic didn't want Jagree to leave school early, but he looked forward to that day when their relationship could be casual again.

The next diary entry was dated a few days later.

> *The' strange'st thing just happe'ne'd. I told a story at an inn, and the'y gave' me' fre'e' suppe'r and a room for the' night! I told the' tale' be'cause' I'd he'ard it for the' first time' the' day be'fore', and I wante'd to find out if the'y kne'w it. It turne'd out it was ne'w to the'm, too. I le'arne'd it from an old man I me't a couple' days ago. I was trave'ling along like' I've' be'e'n doing since' I le'ft Apple'se'e'd, finding work on farms and in little' towns along the' way, going nowhe're' in particular. I was be'twe'e'n towns and didn't se'e' any farms as it was ge'tting dark. I stumble'd on a little' cabin, and in it was a strange' old man. He' le't me' stay the' night, and fe'd me', and told me' storie's I'd ne've'r he'ard be'fore'. I'm sorry I could only re'me'mbe'r one', or maybe' the'y'd give' me' bre'akfast, too! I'm going to gathe'r as much pape'r as I can and write' down the' storie's I he'ar, be'cause' the'y might turn out to be' ne'w in the' ne'xt place'. That will be' my ne'w life'.*

Elic glanced at the next entry, dated four years later. Soorhi must have devoted himself to collecting stories during that time, rather than writing in his diary. Now Elic knew what the stack of notes was, and how old they were. No wonder they were faded and fragile. He put on his coat again and headed for the Blue Heron.

The inn was busier than ever when he got there, but he managed to get Stell's attention.

"It's about Soorhi's notes," he said above the din.

"What about them?"

"He started collecting them when he was only sixteen. They're over seventy years old! Maybe they should be in Jelf's library."

"I promise to keep them safe until I'm finished," Stell said. "Then Jelf can have them, along with my stories. Can I get you anything?"

Elic chuckled. "I'd better not. I was up too late last night. Looks like you're doing a roaring trade, though. Jagree says you've even got overnight guests." He scanned the crowded room and picked out four unfamiliar faces.

Stell followed his gaze. "It's good for me to keep busy, now that he's gone." Her face paled a moment, then reddened. She looked at Elic with wide eyes. "Crane, I mean. And Ketty. She's gone, too."

"Auntie Stell, do you feel all right?" Elic asked. It was understandable for her to miss her son, but that didn't explain the almost horrified look on her face. "Has anyone made trouble tonight?"

She waved away his concern. "I'm fine. It's just warm in here." She gave him a half smile and fanned her face with her hand. "I'm going to miss Ketty's help, though."

"She made a real impression on Jagree. I wish I could have met her. Where did Crane meet her?"

"Misty Pass. Do you know where that is?"

"No. I don't know where many places are." He resolved to check the map later.

"Jagree's a great help with the heavy work and the stabling. But if I'm going to have this kind of business, I might need to hire a girl to help out. Do you know of anyone who might want to earn a few duls?"

This proposal so surprised Elic, he couldn't answer right away. A Deep River girl, working at the Blue Heron? It was unheard of! At least, it had been. Other changes had already occurred. Why not this?

"I'll think about it," he said, and turned to leave.

"Before you go, I want to show you something." Stell pulled a folded paper from her apron pocket. "A nice man rode all the way from Oxbow to bring it and wouldn't stay longer than to eat a quick bite."

"What is it?"

She beamed. "A letter! Have you ever seen one? We used to write and receive letters all the time, until ... you know."

"How interesting." He gasped at a sudden hope. "Is it from Crane?"

"No, from Ketty. Do you want to see it?" Stell held out the folded page.

Elic unfolded the paper and read:

Dear Stell,

With the curse lifted, Deep River should receive letters again, so I hope mine is the first. I got back to Misty Pass with no trouble and found a happy surprise — my father married our good friend Nari! I hope that means I can do more healing and less innkeeping.

If you see our friend again, tell him I miss him. Love, Ketty

Elic refolded the letter and handed it back to Stell. "It was thoughtful of her to write," he said. "Is the friend she mentions Crane?" *Our friend* seemed an odd way to refer to someone's own child, but Elic couldn't imagine who else they might know in common.

"Yes, it must be," Stell answered in a rush.

"Do you suppose he'll write, too?" Elic asked.

"I hope so, but ..."

"Would he even think of it?" he finished for her. Like him, Crane had grown up without mail delivery, but unlike Elic, Crane didn't have a sweetheart to write notes to.

"Who writes home from adventures? But I'm sure he will when he gets the chance." Stell smiled bravely. "Good night, Elic. Pleasant dreams."

Elic stepped outside, his mind on dreams and adventures. He tried to imagine the places Crane might go and the people he'd meet. Away from settled places, probably. He might not meet anyone. Then again, he might encounter other adventurers, or swamp people. How exciting!

Outdoors was dark and cold after the warm, bright inn. Before Elic's eyes could adjust, he bumped into someone near the door, and caught whoever it was by the elbows.

"Excuse me, I — oh." He held Sunnea. He dropped his hands to his sides and looked at the ground. "If you're looking for your father, he's inside."

"I'm not looking for my father." She lifted his chin so he had to meet her gaze. "I was looking for you."

Elic didn't know what to say. Before, she had always waited for him to call on her, but now she had come looking for him twice. True, before his illness, he had visited her at least once a day. Did she expect him to resume that pattern? He remained silent and waited for an explanation.

"I hadn't seen you yet today. I thought something might be wrong, but here you are, out having fun." She kept her tone and expression bland. He heard the accusation anyway.

"I wasn't —" he began to protest.

"Will you still come to supper tomorrow night?" she interrupted. "Mother needs to know."

"Yes, of course," he said, without enthusiasm.

"Elic, what's wrong with you?" Sunnea asked, a sting of anger in her voice. "The curse is broken — things are supposed to get better!"

"I don't know. I'm sorry. I just ... I don't want us to make a mistake."

"A mistake? Elic, we've known each other our whole lives! You said you loved me. How can it be a mistake for us to marry, after so long?"

"But the curse ... what if ... I mean ..."

"You're saying you didn't really love me? It was just the curse? So now ..." She stared at him, her eyes narrowed. "It's Kiat, isn't it?"

"What?"

"You'd rather be with Kiat. Why else would she come to school, at her age?"

"What? No! She helps with the little ones, that's all."

She glared at him but didn't comment.

"So, supper tomorrow?" he asked tentatively.

"If you wish. Don't expect me to welcome you." She turned and strode away, with no squeeze of fingers, no kiss on the cheek.

Elic stared after her. As restrained as she was, she'd never left him with nothing. He'd never seen her this angry, either. They'd had minor disagreements, but never a real fight. They always came to an agreement before it went that far. Or rather, she always gave in. Now she argued whenever they met. He wasn't even sure what this fight was about, only that it was his fault. It wasn't fair. He was thinking of both of them, trying to prevent a mistake that would last the rest of their lives. Why couldn't she understand?

Back home again, Elic got into bed and lay in the dark, his mind on Sunnea. His old feelings for her no longer fit. Why should her anger bother him so much? Yet it did, more than he liked to admit. He didn't know what to make of her new attitude. He found it disturbing ... and intriguing.

Before he slept, he let his mind drift back to his last comfortable moment with her. They sat together on his front step in the cold, the morning the curse was lifted. He'd taken simple pleasure from the warmth of her body next to his. He felt it again now. If he married her, she could warm him every day ... and every night. What could be wrong in that?

He wasn't quite dreaming, but as he drifted, his mind substituted other young women for Sunnea. First Kiat took her place at his side, then her sister Tiek, then Old Myn's daughter Mynna, and finally, Crane's friend,

Ketty. It was unnerving. He liked Kiat, but he'd never thought of her as anything except a classmate or assistant. Likewise Tiek, who was already two years married and a mother. He didn't even like Mynna, and he'd never met Ketty. Yet their warmth, in his imagination, was as pleasant as Sunnea's.

Mutual comfort might be a valid reason to marry. It was no reason to marry Sunnea, in particular. Was it enough that he had loved her once? He would have said then he knew her well, which should count for something. Now he wasn't even sure about that.

Chapter 8. A Break

The next morning, Elic posted the map on the wall — one new thing. "Who can find Misty Pass on the map?"

Jagree volunteered to try, and after a brief search, located the village in the heart of the mountains. "Is it a big town?"

"I don't know," Elic replied. "It's probably not a city, but it might be larger than Deep River."

"That isn't saying much."

"Why is this Misty Pass place so important?" Lafa asked.

"I'm not sure it is. We're all guessing. But what do you think this is?" Elic pointed to the thick black line that linked several towns and villages across the map and reached all the way to Eukard City. Lafa shook his head.

"A road?" Jagree guessed.

Elic gave his brother an approving smile. "Yes! This looks like the main east-west route across Eukard. It connects Eukard City with all the places over here."

"What does the city need with us?" Alryg asked.

"Excellent question," Elic said. "Any guesses?"

They puzzled in silence for a time. Finally, Rynk, who had been quiet until now, spoke up. "Taxes?"

"Good! The tax gatherer has to get around easily, so that's an important reason for the connecting road. Soorhi told me another reason. There used to be large fruit orchards all along the river. Maybe Deep River sent fruit and other farm produce to the city."

"What do we get out of it?" Lafa asked.

"Besides money for the crops? I don't know, but let's think. What can't we make or grow ourselves?"

The list they came up with wasn't long — Deep River had grown self-sufficient under the curse — but it included such things as window glass, sugar, and new settlers.

"So that main road is important. There are other roads." He pointed out a few, including the one running through Deep River. "But not many passes through the mountains. All the other roads join the main road before it reaches the pass. Everyone who travels across the mountains has to go through Misty Pass. It must be an interesting place."

The geography lesson improved Elic's mood. The broken curse continued as a topic of interest in both classes, less urgent than it had been. Kiat did not visit the afternoon class this time. Although Elic missed her assistance, he was just as glad not to see her so soon after Sunnea's unfounded accusations. He helped the youngest students himself while the older girls worked together on their lessons. Everyone was back to the routine of reading, writing, and figures. Elic still wondered whether any of this would benefit the children in the long run. They enjoyed it for now, and it took his mind off his troubles.

After a day spent thinking about Misty Pass and all the other unknown towns on the map, Deep River seemed duller than before. Under the curse, nothing happened and nothing changed. The main difference now, as far as Elic could tell, was that he *knew* nothing happened and nothing changed.

There was something new for him to do, though; or something he hadn't done in three months. The weekly market was set up in the field next to the Village Hall. After school, Elic visited the market to buy or trade for the things he needed if he was going to cook for himself. He took his money bag and a pail of apples — apples that would have gone unpicked if it had been left to Elic. They had ripened over a month back, when it had been an effort to even get out of bed. Mam and Jagree had done most of the harvesting, though they had persuaded Elic to come out and pick a few. Being outdoors, working at a task, he had felt almost himself, at least for a short time. Fortunately, the apples were good keepers. Elic had shared them widely and still had plenty for himself.

Winter markets were smaller and quieter than in summer, the last time Elic had visited. Local farmers sold meat and produce from their wagons, and a few of the town's craftspeople shivered in booths behind their wares. Music filled the air, adding liveliness to the chilly afternoon. It must have been the group Jagree had mentioned.

By the time Elic arrived, the sun was about to set. He hurried to make his purchases before everyone packed up. He traded apples for bunches of kale, a small sack of barley, and a chunk of pork shoulder. He was about to leave when the low sun shone through a gap in the clouds and glinted off a display. A stranger — a stranger! — sat at the table, smiling as he caught Elic's eye. He had dark hair and light skin like many people in Deep River, but his wide nose and arched eyebrows were not those of any of the families Elic knew.

"Something pretty for your sweetheart?" the man asked.

Elic wasn't about to explain to a stranger everything going on with Sunnea. Maybe a gift would help smooth things over. He had to admit he didn't know whether he wanted that, but he'd never spoken to a stranger before. Something else new. He stepped up to the table.

"What does she like?" the merchant asked. "A bracelet, perhaps? Or a ring?"

"I ... don't know," Elic replied. He had never seen Sunnea wear this kind of decorative object. "Maybe something like this?" He picked up a silver pin, a spray of three blossoms, each with a small blue stone in the center. It reminded him of her summer scent and would look nice pinned to her blue cloak. "Are they roses?"

"Apple blossoms, but you have a good eye, my friend," the merchant said. "That brooch was crafted by a master silversmith in Eukard City, and those are fine sapphires from Azzar."

Elic knew little of either place. He tried to picture them on the map. The rest of the world was coming to Deep River and he couldn't do anything about it.

Apple blossoms, though. When Elic had proposed marriage, Sunnea had said she wanted the wedding to be in apple blossom time. Giving her this pin would show her he had been listening. "They might be too fine for my purse," he said. "How much is it?"

"I would usually ask ten duls, but for a man of taste such as yourself," the merchant tapped his chin, "eight."

Elic had never spent eight duls all at once before, but the man made it sound like a bargain. And it was a lovely bauble. He could give it to Sunnea at supper and win her back. He handed over the coins. "Thank you. That's very kind." He slipped the pin into his pocket and returned home as the sun slid behind the mountains.

In the evening, Elic prepared for the betrothal supper. They had put it off for too long already. If he tried to delay or cancel it now, Sunnea would end things for good. Maybe that would be for the best, but Elic didn't want to break their betrothal in haste, any more than he wanted to marry in haste. His idle thoughts still pictured the life they would have together, thoughts that warmed his heart as they always had. If he could get through this supper without embarrassing either of them in front of their parents, there would be time to calmly think and talk things through before they committed to a spring wedding.

He washed and dressed with elaborate care. His hands shook as he buttoned his best shirt, and his heart throbbed as if he were calling on Sunnea for the first time. He felt like a fraud, going through the ritual when he wasn't sure he could go through with the marriage. He wanted the evening to be over so they could move on to whatever came next.

He passed his parents' house on the way and met Jagree as he crossed the road to the inn. "You're all dressed up," Jagree said. "All this just for supper?"

"It's an important occasion," Elic replied. "You'll understand someday."

Jagree laughed. "Not likely. Have fun!"

Elic left his brother still chuckling and continued to his destination. Sunnea's father, Yshna, opened the door as soon as Elic knocked. "Welcome, my boy, come in!" he cried, and ushered Elic into the front room.

Yshna's short stature was exaggerated by a slight stoop. His thinning hair was still dark, and Ati made sure it was neatly trimmed. Like most men in Deep River, he was clean-shaven. He had a milder personality than his wife and kept the peace by going along. Elic had thought Sunnea took after her father in that regard, though now he wasn't sure. He recalled Yshna's outburst at the inn. Maybe Sunnea was like him after all.

Yshna's tailoring workshop was dark, but the rest of the front room was warm and bright with lamplight. The table had been pulled out of the kitchen into this pleasant sitting room for the occasion. It was laid for six. Elic's parents stood by, beaming.

"Mam? Pap? I didn't expect to see you tonight," Elic said.

"Why not?" Mam asked. "We're all celebrating the same thing."

"About time, too." Ati emerged from the kitchen. She was both taller and broader than her husband, a handsome but intimidating woman. She wore her gray-streaked brown hair in a tight bun that kept every hair out of her face. She set a platter of fragrant roast chicken on the table, the skin brown and crackling. "I've never known a betrothal party put off so long. It's hardly proper. Yshna, will you bring the vegetables, please?"

With a smile, he went to the kitchen, returning with two bowls, one of carrots and parsnips glistening with butter and sprinkled with dill, the other of cooked greens. Elic caught a bracing vinegar tang from the steaming dish.

The one person Elic didn't see was Sunnea. He remembered what she'd said about not welcoming him. Did she plan to be elsewhere? How could he explain that?

"Where is that girl?" Ati said, before Elic could ask. "In her room, primping, I suppose. I'll call her."

Elic held his breath, but when Ati returned, Sunnea followed her. She wore her best dress, pale blue with darker stripes. Her hair was pulled into a neat bun, too, softened by a few loose curls in the front. The gold rings on her ears glinted in the lamplight. She smiled at Mam and Pap, without any sparkle. She didn't speak as she glanced at Elic.

Ati directed Elic to sit across from Sunnea, who sat between their fathers. Elic's mother sat to his left and Ati to his right.

"I found one bottle of wine down in the cellar, from

the old days," Yshna said. "It seemed appropriate for a special occasion."

Elic had never tasted wine, nor even seen it. His puzzlement must have shown on his face. Pap smiled and offered an explanation.

"They used to grow wine grapes all along the river, until it dried up," he said. "Most of the wine went to the city, but we kept the best vintages here."

"This should be pretty good, if it isn't vinegar," Yshna added, and filled their cups. "To the happy couple."

Everyone raised cups and drank. The wine was dark, strong, and smooth. Elic took this as a hopeful sign, though Sunnea didn't look happy. He was glad when dishes were passed, and they began eating. Food might distract their parents' attention, though he had little appetite himself.

"If you're to be married in the spring, we have a lot of work to do," Ati said. "You'll need a new dress, Sunnea, and all your household things. Then there's the feast to plan and —"

"We might hire musicians," Yshna interrupted. Ati frowned, but he didn't appear to notice. "There was a group at the market today, fiddle, flute, and drums, playing and spreading the word about the winter dance in Bitter Springs."

"The winter dance!" Mam cried. "Remember, Ohme, when we were young, how we'd drive up there? Those were good times."

"And we'd have a summer dance here in Deep River," Yshna added. "Maybe we should start that again."

"Something like that just attracts strangers and troublemakers," Ati objected. "And the young people, staying up till all hours ..."

Her husband and Elic's parents brushed off these objections, recalling dances and other festive occasions in their youth. Elic had never heard these stories — that damned curse again! He enjoyed seeing his mother's face bright with happy memories. His own troubles faded, and he managed to eat a little of the delicious supper. Ati had outdone herself. If Sunnea was half the cook her stepmother was, and the meat pie hinted she was more than that, he would eat well when they ... *if* they married. Maybe that was reason enough. Elic ate another bite of chicken.

"Speaking of troublemakers, Yshna, I hear you almost got into a fight at the inn the other evening," Pap said.

Ati frowned. "We're not talking about *that*."

"It was only a bit of foolishness," Yshna mumbled.

"Not the only one!" Ati sipped her wine and continued. "Yesterday, he suggested we get out the buggy and go for a ride. But we haven't owned a horse in years!"

"There's an obvious solution to that problem," Yshna broke in. "I asked Breff if he had a suitable animal, and he said he did."

"I supposed Breff would bring this horse to town the next time he came in," Ati said, "but the next thing I know, Yshna is sitting in Breff's wagon, on his way to look it over." She drank another mouthful of wine. "What could I do? I went along to make sure he didn't make a foolish deal." She allowed herself a hint of a smile before going on with the story. "We were almost to Breff and Tiek's place when we passed Keena, walking by herself. I asked if she was going to visit her grandbabies, and what do you think?" She paused and gulped more wine, draining her cup. "She said, 'I just want to see where this road goes.' My own brother's wife! Did you ever hear the like?" She sounded scandalized, but she was smiling more than before. Elic had never seen her cheeks so flushed or her eyes so bright.

The others shook their heads and chuckled. Yshna refilled their cups. Elic smiled at Sunnea. She wasn't the only one behaving out of character. She did not return his smile.

She laid down her fork, though she'd barely eaten anything. "May I be excused?"

"But it's your party," Ati said. "Your young man is here."

"I don't feel well," she replied, and left the table.

"It must be the wine. Or nerves," Yshna explained. "Who can blame her?" All but Elic laughed in agreement.

Elic pushed back from the table. "I'd better be going, too. I'll just say good night to Sunnea."

He went to her room and tapped at the door. "It's Elic." There was no reply. "Sunnea, are you all right?" Still no reply. "Please, Sunnea, talk to me."

She opened the door. She still wore her best dress, but her hair was down. Her eyes were red, though she wasn't crying now. She pushed her hair behind her ears. The courtship ring glinted from her right ear. The betrothal ring was gone.

"What?" she said.

Elic stared at her ear and couldn't speak. She started to close the door, but he caught the handle. "Wait. I'm sorry. I haven't been myself, and I've said some foolish things." He fumbled for the pin in his pocket.

"Not so foolish," she said before he could pull it out. "Maybe you were right. We don't want to make a mistake."

He didn't like hearing his own words from her mouth. Had it stung this badly when he said them?

"I never imagined being with anyone else," she continued. "Did you? We just assumed we'd be married someday, as if it had all been arranged by someone else. But I don't want to marry you out of a lack of imagination. Not now. It wouldn't be right."

She was right. And saying it better than Elic had himself. His heart ached all the same. They felt the same way, but it was hard to give up what they'd always looked forward to.

"Maybe we could —"

"Good night, Elic." She closed the door.

When Elic left Sunnea's house, their parents were still celebrating, unaware of the break. He didn't tell them. There was no sense in upsetting everyone.

He went back to his house. The little place seemed lonely in a way it never had before. He'd been planning how to make it more suitable for a wife and family. Now those changes might not be needed. He stood before his shaving glass and looked at the gold betrothal ring in his earlobe. He couldn't be betrothed if she wasn't. He removed it and laid it on the shelf next to his razor, and the little silver pin beside it. Maybe he had loved Sunnea out of habit, but he couldn't imagine marrying anyone else, curse or no curse. He'd end up an old bachelor, like Soorhi.

The thought of Soorhi led him to the diary, a welcome distraction.

Look what I found at the' bottom of my pack! The' diary Clove'r gave' me'. I have'n't thought of he'r or it in a long time', but I'm glad to find it, and I thank he'r in my he'art. She' was ve'ry patie'nt with a young fool. I've' had good luck the'se' past ye'ars, colle'cting obscure' storie's and sharing the'm in othe'r place's. Ne'arly always good for a me'al or a place' to sle'ep! He'rmits have' be'en my be'st source'. They re'mind me' of swamp pe'ople', ke'eping to the'mse'lve's and avoiding the' tax colle'ctor. Maybe' the'y came' from the' same' place', a long time' ago, but found anothe'r way. They ke'ep out of sight but don't move' around. The' diffe're'nce' is, I ne've'r me't one' who didn't we'lcome' me'. I've' be'en spending summe'rs in the' mountains, according to the' advice' of an innke'epe'r in Swe'etwate'r. He' he'ard the're' we're' lots of he'rmits up he're'. So far, I've' had no luck. I don't mind be'ing alone' in the' high place's, though. It's be'autiful whe'n I come' out of thick woods into a blooming me'adow or a whole' slope' of loade'd, ripe' be'rry bushe's. At the' right time' of ye'ar — now — I can pick e'nough be'rrie's to buy me' two or three nights' lodging down below.

It was a strange picture, little old Soorhi hiking those wild slopes, camping out, foraging. Elic had to remind himself yet again that the Soorhi who had written this account had been a young man, around Elic's own age. He sighed. Not a bad idea, to go off into the wilderness and be completely alone. To leave behind the bungled explanations and hurt feelings, the parents who had no idea and the sweetheart who understood only too well. A complete escape.

I've been all alone for weeks now, though at times I was sure there were other people all around me. I never saw anyone until today. I was picking berries, keeping half an eye out for bears, when I saw someone behind me. That often happens — I see what's happening behind my back. It's usually of no consequence, like most of my visions, though always true. Up here, it seemed my mind was playing tricks, and I didn't trust it. I looked anyway, and this time I did see someone standing no more than ten paces from me. How did he get so close without my hearing? He was dark of skin and eyes, with bushy black hair. He looked young — slender build, smooth skin, no gray hair. He might have been my own age, but head and shoulders taller than any man I've ever seen — a giant. Mountain Folk? Though in the stories, they are always portrayed as monsters, and this was a man. Everybody has stories of them, but they always seemed mere tales to frighten children, or stories of long ago. Only the hermits regard them as fact. This giant didn't appear hostile, though when I greeted him, he replied in words I couldn't understand. If they were words. It sounded more like percussive music than language. I wanted to offer some of my berries. When I turned back, he was gone. How can someone so big vanish so completely?

Elic looked up from the diary, breathless. Soorhi had never spoken to him of any of this. He'd had a real adventure and never mentioned it! Elic tried to imagine meeting real, live Mountain Folk. Stell told stories of them; not as if they were real. It seemed impossible Soorhi had met legendary people, but Elic had never known him to invent stories the way Stell did. Something about his description of the giant sounded familiar, though Elic couldn't think why it would. Familiar, and recent. Maybe it would come to him later. He read on.

I went on picking, and the next time I looked up, there were two of them! The second one had straight hair and lighter eyes, but they were

othe'rwise' ide'ntical, at le'ast to my eye's. They wore'
de'e'rskin clothing, dapple'd to ble'nd with shade', and
soft shoe's. The'se' pe'ople' know how to hide'. The'
first one' pointe'd at himself and said, as be'st I could
make' out, "Aklaka," the'n at me' and said some'thing
similar that I didn't quite' catch. It sounde'd like' an
introduction, so I pointe'd to myself and said my
name', the'n to him and said, "Aklaka." Whe'n I
ge'sture'd at his frie'nd, he' said "Aklaka," too. I
ne've'r thought about diffe're'nt language's be'fore'. It
is difficult to communicate' whe'n you don't spe'ak
the' same' one'. Afte'r se've'ral atte'mpts, I figure'd out
"Aklaka" was not his name', but the' name' of his
pe'ople', what the' Mountain Folk call the'mse'lve's.
The' othe'r word must me'an e've'ryone' e'lse', not just
me'. They trie'd to te'll me' the'ir own name's, too.
They we're' long and impossible' for me' to
pronounce'. I calle'd the'm "Bushy" and
"Lighteye's." They took me' with the'm to the'ir
camp, whe're' the're' we're' two othe'rs, who I call
"Scar" and "Whiske'rs." It looks like' a fish-
smoking ope'ration, though we' all share'd one' big
salmon fre'sh, with some' of my be'rrie's. They have'
appare'ntly adopte'd me', I don't know whe'the'r as
brothe'r or pe't. But they are' good nature'd. They
laugh a lot and play little' game's as they work. They

are' all watching me' write' this and se'em fascinate'd.
Maybe' they don't write'? They sing the'ir storie's.
I wish I could unde'rstand.

Elic hated to stop in the middle of this episode, but it was late, and his eyes kept drooping closed. He marked the place and closed the diary. As he prepared for bed, he considered the description of the Aklaka man called Bushy. Why would it seem familiar? The only tall, dark person Elic knew was Crane. He was more like the one called Lighteyes, if anyone. An odd thought — Crane, one of the Mountain Folk? Elic remembered Jagree's description of the stranger at the inn. Hadn't he said, *darker than Crane* and *wild, bushy hair*? And there was Stell's odd behavior whenever she spoke of her mysterious guest.

Elic left off puzzling and lay down to sleep. He dreamed many things that night. He dreamed he was a hermit and Soorhi was looking for him but couldn't find him. He dreamed he stood at Sunnea's door. She wouldn't let him in. Finally, he dreamed Crane sat in Stell's rocker and sang a story, while Stell lurked in the shadows with someone Elic couldn't see. What — or who — was she hiding?

Chapter 9. Letters

It snowed during the night, and by morning, every bare branch of Elic's apple tree was lined with white. Big wet flakes continued to fall as he trudged to school. The snow was deep enough on the path to roll into balls ahead of his boot toes. As he opened the schoolhouse door, a larger snowball splattered against the back of his head and dribbled down his neck. He turned, brushing chunks of snow out of his hair. Jagree grinned at him from the road.

"That's quite an arm you've got there," Elic said.

"Why so early?"

"Helping Stell." Jagree joined him on the step and stamped the snow off his boots. "She had guests leaving early, so I got their horses ready."

Horses. That explained the grin, aside from the accurately thrown snowball. At least one of them was happy.

"It's getting so busy at the Heron, I could quit school and work for Stell full-time!"

"You're a blacksmith, not an innkeeper," Elic objected.

"We'll see."

Elic didn't know how to respond. Stell had said Jagree was helpful and that she could use an extra pair of hands. But Jagree had never wanted to be anything except a blacksmith, at least since he was old enough to understand he couldn't be a horse. He'd been learning the trade for close to three years, and according to Pap, had a real talent for it. With practice, he was growing both strong and skilled. Why would he consider a different trade now? Elic already knew the answer. The same reason he would consider breaking with Sunnea.

"May I ask you something?"

"Of course, Teacher," Jagree replied. He sat on a bench, folded his hands on the desk, and looked up at Elic with an impertinent grin.

"Not as your teacher, as your brother." Elic gave Jagree's shoulder a light shove. "The stranger you and Ketty brought to the inn — did you notice anything about him?"

Jagree frowned. "Like what?"

"Anything different." Elic didn't want to be more

explicit. How would Jagree know whether the man resembled Mountain Folk, after all? "Did he look like a normal man?"

"A normal man? Sure." Jagree nodded. "But he didn't look like anyone from around here, if that's what you mean."

"Was he tall? As tall as Crane? Maybe taller?"

"I never saw him standing, but maybe. I only saw him awake one time, and only for a moment." He frowned in thought. "You might say his eyes were unusual."

"Really? How so?" Elic asked.

"They were deep blue. I'm not sure I've ever seen eyes quite that color."

That wasn't what Elic expected. It didn't tell him whether the stranger was a giant or not. Could a giant have blue eyes? In Stell's stories, they had eyes like black pits or yellow fire. Those were made-up monsters, not Soorhi's Aklaka. Yet something about Jagree's observation seemed familiar. From a story, maybe. Before he could consider the matter, the rest of the class arrived, laughing and stamping snow from their boots.

As they took their seats, Jagree said, "I found out what that fellow from Oxbow brought to Stell."

"I know," Elic said. "A letter. She let me read it."

"It doesn't make sense. Who does she know in Oxbow?"

"No one. It was from Ketty."

The color rose in Jagree's face. "What's she doing there?" he asked.

By now the rest of the class was listening. Elic hadn't intended to teach a lesson on this subject, but he had their attention, and they might need this information someday. "Class, today's first lesson concerns mail service. Deep River has been cut off for a long time. Now that Yrae's Curse has been lifted, things can go back to how they used to be. We're all too young to remember, but our parents and grandparents knew a time when people left Deep River for other places or moved here from somewhere else."

"Why?" Lafa asked. Alryg laughed, and Lafa flushed with embarrassment.

"That's a perfectly good question, Lafa," Elic said, and frowned at the others. "It's hard to understand something you've never seen. Let's think about it. A man might like the look of the land and wish to settle there. A woman might marry a man from another town and move away with him. A family might want a new start in a new place. But there are still friends and relations in the old place. How do you keep in touch?" He waited a moment. No one offered an answer. "You write a letter," he said at last.

"I thought letters were for sweethearts," Jagree said with a sly grin.

Elic blushed. He had believed, foolishly it seemed, his many notes to Sunnea had been secret. He hadn't written one in months; not since they had officially begun courting in the spring. Maybe if he wrote to her again, it would help them find their way back to the old sweet and simple bond. If that was what either of them wanted now.

During class was not the time to solve that mystery. "That's a different kind of letter," Elic said. "But in either case, you write down what you can't say aloud. If you can get it to a coach stop, the coach can carry it along the route and deliver it near its destination. If it has to go somewhere off the route, they have riders who'll take it."

"You still haven't explained why Ketty is in Oxbow," Jagree said.

"She isn't. She wrote the letter in Misty Pass and put it on the coach there. Oxbow is the nearest coach stop to Deep River, so that's where the rider came from."

He let Jagree explain about the rider and the coaches. He sounded like an expert already and actually was one on the subject of the rider's sorrel mare. The whole class was engaged by this lesson, mundane as the subject was. But it was new to them. Even though none of them knew anyone outside Deep River, a lesson on mail service held them more than another lesson in grammar. Perhaps there were more lessons he could teach about this new world. It might keep them in school another year or two. Because someday soon, they probably would know someone who had left Deep River — or leave it themselves.

The snow had stopped by the end of the morning. A heavy blanket of it lay over everything. The boys burst outside after class and immediately started a snowball fight. Elic watched from the relative safety of the doorway. Lafa was the most accurate, but Jagree threw harder. Elic resisted the urge to join in, though he had a good arm, too. He had to act like an adult, even if he didn't always feel like one. And they would all be soaked by the time they got home. He preferred to stay dry.

He had time before the afternoon class to go home and eat lunch, the remains of Sunnea's meat pie. Mixed feelings about the cook did not prevent him from savoring the meal. While he ate, he picked up Soorhi's diary again and continued where he had left off the previous night.

They sing their stories. I wish I could understand. That would be a real accomplishment, to collect the stories of the Mountain Folk. I'd get more than supper and a night's lodging for that! If anyone believed me, that is. I've met few people who've even caught a glimpse of one. They're more secretive than swamp people! I wish I could ask why.

The next entry was dated a few days later:

I'm alone again. After four days with the Aklaka, I was feeling comfortable and even beginning to understand a word or two: fish, fire, stream. They call the biggest peak Aku. The young men were usually talkative and laughing. A couple of them spent long periods every day sitting very still and — this is my best guess — listening. I tried it and didn't hear anything unusual, but I had a vision that was clearer and lasted longer than any I've had before. Everything was going well, and I thought I was becoming one of them. Until yesterday, when Scar ran into camp, excited about something. Bushy looked alarmed and made me hide under a pile of branches. I lay still and didn't make a sound but watched through a gap in the twigs. Soon, a whole crowd of women and children reached the camp. I'm sure some of the women were my friends' mothers, by the way they fussed over them. And there was one tall, beautiful girl, maybe sixteen years old, who resembled Bushy, except with straight hair. His sister? She looked right at me, or at least, right at my hiding spot. How I longed to meet her! I'm sure I could learn a new language for someone like that. They stayed a while, then gathered all the smoked fish and continued on their way. Bushy and friends did not seem as cheerful when they dug me out of hiding. Then I saw it, not a vision, but just as plain — these four took me in out of curiosity, and maybe rebellion. They didn't want their mothers to know. I won't go home with them to meet their families, their sisters ... Just when I was thinking we weren't so different. But I am still an outsider. I am alone again, with a story I can't tell. Summer is ending. It is time to come down from the mountains, anyway.

Elic was caught up in Soorhi's tale and wanted to know what came next, but he had to leave the story there and return to school for the afternoon class. As he set the diary aside, he wondered why Soorhi had never shared any of his own adventures. Surely his own story was as exciting as any of the tales he'd collected. Elic could understand that he hadn't told about the Mountain Folk out of respect for their privacy, but he'd had other experiences besides. Then again, he came from secretive people himself, even if he'd left them at an early age. Maybe he never lost the habit.

Back in school, Elic presented the same lesson to the afternoon class he had to the older boys in the morning. While the young children were not particularly interested in mail service, the older girls grasped the concept immediately. Though none of them had ever been more than a short distance from Deep River and didn't know people in other places, they all understood what it would feel like to be separated from family and friends. Of course one would wish to share news with loved ones who had left home.

"Think of it!" Kiat cried. She was back after the one day away, though Elic did not believe he was the cause of it, whatever Sunnea said. There must be another reason. "You could go traveling and write home about all the interesting things you were doing and the unusual things you'd seen."

The rest of the class seemed startled, as if they hadn't considered the possibility of leaving home themselves. But Kiat had. That was interesting. She was lively and smart, and as pretty as Sunnea, in a different way. She was shorter, with a curvier form and brown hair and eyes. She'd had a few suitors since she received her courtship ring. Elic didn't know whether any of her fellows had proposed marriage. She would see someone once or twice, then take up with someone else. She had a reputation as something of a tease, but none of the men who'd gone walking with Kiat spoke ill of her. She was like Stell in that regard, which gave Elic an idea.

"Kiat, could you stay a moment?" he asked as the rest of the class left at the end of the day. She returned to his desk and waited, smiling. After the door closed behind a departing student, Elic cleared his throat. "Kiat, I was wondering ... would you be interested —"

"In going walking with you? Of course! If Sunnea won't mind?"

That wasn't what he'd intended to ask, but now she'd brought it up, the idea interested him. He needed someone his own age to talk to — someone besides Crane or Sunnea. He could tell her about Stell's proposal, maybe share some of his own troubles. "Sunnea wants to think things over." He touched his left earlobe, naked without the earring. Kiat's eyes followed his finger.

"How about tonight?" she responded without further hesitation.

"To-tonight?" he stammered.

"The sky should be clear, and the snow will be beautiful with the moon shining on it. Stop by after supper. Dress warm!"

Chapter 10. A Walk in the Moonlight

After school, Elic walked to the Village Hall. The sun was setting, but Jelf was still in the library, finishing his day's work. He squinted at Elic, then greeted him with a smile. "Is this going to be a regular thing now?"

"Maybe. The children are curious about what Deep River was like before the curse, and what it might be like again. I've been guessing, but it's time to find answers. Mam suggested I look in the old logs."

"I'd be glad to share them with you. It's been a long time since anyone besides me opened them." Jelf gestured toward the top shelf, where the logs resided. "Where do you want to start?"

"I don't know — the beginning?" Jelf pointed him to the earliest volume. Elic lifted it down and blew the dust off it. It was a much larger book than Soorhi's diary. They had in common yellowed pages and faded ink. The first entry was dated over a hundred years ago.

We have reached our appointed townsite at last. It seems a lifetime since we left Eukard City to help settle this new territory, though in reality it has been mere weeks. Tents and sod huts will shelter us until we can build something permanent. There are almost no trees, except a few near the river. We will have to build with stones — they, at least, are plentiful. We are lucky to have a skilled mason among us. It will be hard work starting a town and farms, but the party is in hopeful spirits. There is good land and plenty of water, and the town will be in a pleasant spot. We voted to name the town Deep River.

- Fajel, Keeper

Elic had never heard of Fajel before. It was odd to see a name other than Jelf with the title of Keeper. "Jelf, who was this Fajel?"

"My grandfather," Jelf replied. "He had the most

schooling, so they appointed him Keeper first thing."

"I wish there was a record from before this. He talks about settling new territory, but not about why."

"Then you're in luck. None of it is written down, but I grew up hearing stories about the founders and settlement. Do you have plans tonight?"

Elic thought of his plans with Kiat. Jelf didn't need to know that. "Not until after supper."

"Good. Let's go over to the Heron, and I'll tell you what I remember."

Elic wasn't interested in cooking supper for himself, so this idea suited him. It was a lot of trouble to make something that tasted good — too much trouble for one person. His mother was always happy to cook for him, though then he felt like a child. A grown man could eat at the Heron.

The place was busy, with local people as well as strangers. Rovhi and Huvro, farm brothers near Elic's age, listened with rapt attention as a traveler spun a tale. A small, silver-haired man sat by himself near the door. He wore an eyepatch and would have looked alarming, had he not smiled at Jelf as they entered. Jelf greeted him, and Elic smiled politely, though he had never seen the man before.

"This is Fane, a traveling herbalist," Jelf said. "Fane, this is Elic, our teacher. His mother is the town midwife. You'll want to meet her tomorrow."

Elic shook Fane's hand, then found a place across from Jelf at one of the long tables. "Fane came by the Hall late this afternoon, just before you did," Jelf explained. "I told him he was late for this week's market day, but he should talk to Sudi in the morning. A fascinating fellow."

Stell swept over and interrupted their talk. "Supper tonight?"

"Yes, please," Elic said.

She smiled at him. "Are you staying for stories, Elic?"

"No, I have other ... business."

She glanced at his naked ear and frowned but didn't comment. He knew he could confide in her if he wished — she could keep a secret. He would have to wait until they were alone. "What about you, Jelf?" she asked.

"I might stay for a few." As she walked away, he turned to Elic. "How far back do you want to go?"

"Like I said before, the beginning. What did Fajel mean by 'settle this new territory'?"

"To explain that I'll have to go back a long way," Jelf said. "A long time ago, hundreds of years now, the last king of Eukard settled an old dispute with the neighboring land of Azzar."

"Never heard of Azzar before yesterday," Elic said. "Now here it is again, but I still don't know anything about it."

"Then it's time you did. It's our neighbor to the east. Foryin is to the south. I expect we'll be hearing more about them in the coming years, now that we're back in touch with the rest of the world. Eukard and Azzar had a long-running dispute over the territory between them. King Braffin met with Empress Zelleen of Azzar, and they worked out a treaty that split the disputed territory between them. The Treaty of the Waters. Eukard gained all the land from the mountains to the Great River. There was almost nobody living here, though, and it stayed that way for a long time. Some folk grazed sheep here and there, and there were tales of Mountain Folk foraging and hunting, but you can't believe everything you hear."

Elic didn't interrupt, though his heart raced at the mention of Mountain Folk. He enjoyed knowing something Jelf didn't.

"So finally, one of the early governors sent out a few hardy souls to explore, and they came back with reports of fertile land, just waiting to be farmed, rivers of water, a pleasant climate, and so on. Before long, little bands of settlers were heading over the pass."

"This sounds like a story I should know," Stell said as she served them ale and bowls of hearty beef stew with carrots, onions, and potatoes.

"When you finish writing yours down, I'll share it with you," Jelf promised.

"Why would people want to settle in a place they'd never seen?" Elic asked.

"I expect some went for the adventure of it," Jelf said. "And others, for the dry climate. Some were probably tired of city life and city ways. The farmers who went might have been workers who wanted a chance to have their own land, or people wanting a fresh start after hard times. It probably wasn't that easy here, but with a little water, they found this soil could grow just about anything. Close to the river, they planted apples and cherries and wine grapes, and farther out, wheat and oats and barley."

Without the river, nobody grew fruit crops anymore. The grain crops were familiar. As Elic considered this, Mayor Myn entered. He stared suspiciously at the strangers, then sat next to Elic, as if placing him between himself and the outsiders.

"What I want to know is, when will things go back to how they were?" Old Myn said, as if he and Elic had already been conversing.

"Pardon?" Elic's imagination was still filled with the founders settling new territory. "How they were when?"

"Before. Somebody said we were under a curse, but I call it a blessing that keeps their sort out and our sort in!" He tilted his head toward Fane and the traveler who regaled the young men.

Elic wasn't sure how to answer. Stell saved him the trouble. As she set down another mug of ale, she gave Myn her brightest smile. "Good evening, Mayor. It's always an honor to serve such a distinguished guest. How's your daughter?"

Since the day Sunnea mentioned her, Elic hadn't given much thought to Mynna — until she popped into his daydream. It was hard to imagine her a farmer's wife with a husband a decade older, but she must have had her reasons for accepting Brak.

"There's another thing," Myn grumbled. "Who's to take care of me now? What kind of daughter leaves her widowed father to take care of himself?"

"And a little boy," Stell added. "Where is Young Myn tonight?"

"I sent him over to Farl and Lynka's for the night. Their Foli is the same age; they'll hardly notice another one."

Stell met Elic's gaze over Myn's head. Without saying a word, he was sure they agreed Mynna had done well to get out of her father's house by any means. But he would keep a closer eye on Young Myn, to make sure he wasn't neglected.

Elic finished his supper and drained his mug. "I'd like to hear more of your thoughts sometime," he said to Myn, glad now he had an appointment to keep, "but I have to go. Thanks, Jelf. We'll talk more later."

He left Jelf listening to Myn's complaints and walked up the road toward Kiat's house. He almost changed his mind. Although there was nothing wrong in meeting with a friend to offer her a job and maybe talk about everything that had happened since the curse lifted, it seemed vaguely improper to visit another girl so soon after breaking with Sunnea. He wasn't courting Kiat, though anyone who saw them would probably assume he was. But things were changing fast in Deep River, and in a way, Sunnea had given him both permission and opportunity to find out how he really felt. He passed Mam and Pap's place at a fast walk, as guilty as if he'd done something wrong. No one tried to stop him, and when he reached Kiat's, he found her waiting on the step.

"Ready?" she asked. "Let's go."

He gestured toward the house. "Shouldn't I speak to Briato first?"

"No." She stepped down beside him.

"Your folks don't want to know who you're with?"

"I'm sure they would, but it's none of their business. I'm of age."

Though the sun was long down, the night was bright. The sky had cleared, and the moon, a day or so past full, shone on the glistening snow. The sky was a deep, clear blue.

Their boots crunched through the frozen crust,

breaking the silence. "You're full of talk," Kiat teased.

"I'm sorry. I don't know what I'm doing with you."

"Walking. Possibly courting?"

"I wasn't thinking that way," Elic admitted. "But is that what you want?"

She laughed and the sound rang through the cold, still air. "Not really. I like attention, something new and exciting. And I like you, Elic. You're the brother I should have had. But I can't imagine settling down with someone I've known all my life."

He echoed her laughter. "What choice do we have?"

"I don't know, but I aim to find out!"

A huge weight lifted from Elic's shoulders. He had been right about needing a friend he could talk to. "You'd leave Deep River?"

"Maybe. I'd love to visit other places."

"Have you really given it serious thought?"

"I wouldn't say serious. Not yet. I've had the dream for a long time, though. I used to think there was something wrong with me."

"That was Yrae's Curse," Elic said. "I thought I was the only one who felt that way."

"You dream of adventure? You always seemed so settled."

"That was before." He whirled to face her and grabbed both her hands, filled with the urgency of a new idea. "Let's go, tonight! We could leave here and ..." He trailed off as she shook her head.

"You have unfinished business here." Kiat withdrew her hands from his. They walked on.

Elic sighed. "I don't know how to finish it. I loved Sunnea for a long time, and maybe I still do. How do I know it wasn't just Yrae's Curse?"

"Could the curse do that? Make you believe you loved someone when you really didn't?"

"I don't know, and I don't know how to find out. Sunnea told me Crane figured out that his presence — his magic, I guess — shielded the people closest to him from the effects of the curse. I should have felt it less than most, but I ended up feeling it more. All because of one adventure. You'd think I would have lost my taste for it."

"It's interesting how you keep mentioning Sunnea to me," Kiat said with a small knowing smile.

"I'm sorry. That's rude, isn't it, to take you out and talk about someone else?"

"I'm not offended." Kiat shrugged. "I can tell when a heart belongs to someone else."

Elic took a deep breath to calm himself. "What I meant to ask you was, would you consider working for Stell at the Heron? She asked me to find her someone, and I thought of you."

Kiat looked so startled he was sure he had offended her this time. She smiled and slowly nodded her head. "I'll consider it. It would get me out of the house. Away from Ma." She shivered.

"Is your mother so hard to live with?"

"Why do you think I help out at school so often? Or Tiek married the first man to ask? There's no way we could live up to Ma's housekeeping standards. Of course, she'd hate it if I went anywhere near the inn." She frowned, then brightened. "I'd say that's a reason in favor! And I could earn my own money, in case I do decide to leave town."

Elic grinned. "I never knew you were so rebellious."

Kiat returned the smile. "I feel sorry for Brynnit, taking all Ma's criticism alone, but I think this is something I could do."

Without paying attention to where they were, they had walked past the school and beyond the edge of town. "Come on, we should go back," Kiat said. She took his gloved hand in her mittened one, and they turned back along the road. Talking wasn't necessary. They had an understanding.

Covered in snow and gleaming in moonlight, the familiar landscape looked strange. Elic had never noticed before how the low hills on either side sloped down to the flat bottom of a valley, with the river at its center. The Mountain shone against the deep blue sky, its eternal white joined to the snow on which Elic stood. For a chilling moment, he saw, not a valley, but a vast river that flowed out from the mountain and swept away everything in its path. Beside him, Kiat shivered.

In the shadows of the Village Hall, she stopped and turned him to face her. "Thank you for taking me walking on such a beautiful night." She stood on tiptoes and kissed him on the lips. Whether it was the ale or the novelty, his whole body tingled. He felt warm now, the chilling vision all but forgotten. Sunnea had often kissed his cheek. She had always been too proper to kiss his lips. He had never insisted, though now he wondered why not.

"Thank *you*." He tried to return the favor.

Kiat pulled away. "No, that's all you get. We won't be walking out again."

"Are you sure?" Elic still needed someone to talk to,

even if it didn't include kisses.

"You're not the one I'm looking for." They continued toward her house. "I've watched you and Sunnea for years. Maybe you can't see it now, but you had something special. And you could have it again."

Kiat's words sounded true. Elic wanted them to be true. He pondered them as he walked home and while he prepared for the next day. As well as porridge oats in the small pot, he put some beans to soak in the big one — he needed to start feeding himself. He kept thinking about Kiat's words after he went to bed. *You had something special. You could have it again.* He could write that in a note to Sunnea. Maybe it would change her mind, at least enough to listen to what he had to say.

When he closed his eyes, he felt Kiat's lips against his, and pretended the lips were Sunnea's.

Chapter II. Returning Dreams

Elic walked in the moonlight, a young woman at his side. Not Kiat this time. Sunnea.

"Thank you for this," he said. "It will give us a chance to talk."

"That's all we do anymore. We need to finish it."

We will, he said, though not aloud. He knew it was true, but not what it meant. They walked on. No one talked. The moon shone bright on the snow, though Elic couldn't find it in the sky.

"It's too cold out," Sunnea said. "Let's go home."

"We can't talk at your house. We'll go to mine."

"No. Not after dark. It wouldn't be proper. Let's go to the haunted house."

Elic had to laugh. It was the last place he expected Sunnea to suggest. At least in warm weather, the so-called haunted house was a favorite courting spot. The spooky atmosphere was supposed to make your sweetheart fall into your arms.

"How is that any more proper?" he asked. "We'd still be alone together, after dark."

"No one would look for us there."

Sunnea was probably right about that. Elic and his mother were the only ones unafraid to go inside. The next moment, they stood on the doorstep, a white stone swept clear of snow and shining in the moonlight. "It isn't really haunted, you know," Elic said. "That's just a tale. It was my Grammy's house."

"Why do they call it haunted, then?"

"Grammy Elika was a witch. Maybe somebody saw something strange once."

He opened the door and led her inside. The house was empty except for a high-backed bench in front of the fireplace. A cheerful blaze crackled in the hearth. Sunnea sat and held her hands out to the warmth. Elic sat beside her and began to speak his carefully chosen words.

"We should marry before the dumpling harvest," he said. "A child is coming to plant the sweet peas. Her name is Sulika."

"Yes, I see," Sunnea said, won over by his eloquence. "Sulika — what a pretty name." She leaned close to kiss him, but before their lips met, a third voice interrupted.

"I'm glad to see you're working things out." Grammy Elika stood before them, her gray-streaked black hair loose around her shoulders. Her thin face could look severe, though now she smiled.

Sunnea shrank back. "But you're dead!"

"A house isn't haunted just because a dead person lives there," Elic said. It seemed reasonable to him. Sunnea jumped up from the bench and fled. Elic stared after her.

Elika studied him. "You're enchanted."

"No, that's past."

Elic's own mumbling voice woke him. He sat up, blinking. It was morning.

"A dream. I should have known."

He remembered how the dream felt, even as it faded. Had he really called Grammy Elika a witch? No one in the family called her that. It was regarded as an insult. She was a magical healer, though, with enough power to intimidate the sort of man who didn't respect women. Had she brought Elic and Sunnea together? He did not usually put much store in dreams or even remember them. Some people believed they carried messages or told the future, like Soorhi's visions.

Elic tried to remember his eloquent words that had persuaded Sunnea, but the few he could recall made no sense. What was a dumpling harvest? *Sulika* was a pretty name, though. Soon, even these fragments faded in the light of day. The feeling remained of how right it felt to be with Sunnea: walking in the moonlight, sitting together and talking things through, working things out. When Elic was with her, at least in his dreams, he was enchanted. Elika had that right. Not cursed. Enchanted.

Elic spent the whole morning alert and on edge. Walking and talking with a woman, whether awake or in dreams, was almost too stimulating. He enjoyed the feeling. It was nothing like talking to Crane or Jagree. Kiat's kiss probably had something to do with it. But she was correct — they weren't right for each other. He needed to tell Sunnea clearly what had happened to him and why he had wanted to break with her. It couldn't be too late to reconcile.

He walked to Sunnea's house between classes. It was still cold, but sunny. Icicles dripped along the south-facing eaves, pitting the snow beneath them.

Ati answered Elic's knock.

"Hello, Elic. I'm glad you've decided to behave properly, " she said, primly.

"I'm not sure I understand," he replied, careful to maintain a polite tone. Did she know about the haunted house? No, that was only a dream.

"Coming to see Sunnea, rather than letting her seek you out," Ati said. "I don't hold with that sort of thing."

"Yes, I see. May I speak to Sunnea, please?"

"I'll call her. Come in and shut the door."

He followed her inside. Yshna sat sewing by a sunny window. He smiled at Elic through a mouthful of pins and said, "Take off your coat," without dropping one. Elic took off his coat and held it until Ati returned with Sunnea.

"You see, dear? Here he is," Ati was saying as the women entered the room. "He hasn't broken with you, so you can forget all that nonsense." She took Elic's coat and hung it up, then sat beside her husband and began to hem a garment. "You two can go into the kitchen, if you want privacy."

"Thank you, we will," Elic said.

"No, that won't be necessary," Sunnea said at the same time. She blushed and looked away. "Oh, all right!" She led Elic to the kitchen. She closed the door behind them and turned to face him, her arms crossed. "What do you want?"

"I was hoping you'd go out walking with me. Perhaps tonight?"

She raised her eyebrows. "Don't you think it's too soon? We broke off our engagement only two days ago."

"I know. It feels longer. I need to talk to you."

She folded her arms. "Then talk."

"I meant, away from parents," he whispered. "To see if we could start over. I don't want to be an old bachelor like Soorhi!"

"I'm sure you won't be. Maybe you should see someone else before you start over with me."

"I tried that."

She stared at him. "Already? You couldn't even wait a day?"

"You said you didn't want to see me."

"I know, but Elic, there are ... proprieties."

"You sound like your mother!"

She turned away. Elic wanted to kick himself. He'd come to make peace, but they were already arguing. Everything he said came out wrong. It had been so much easier in his dream.

"So, who was she?" Sunnea asked.

He hadn't meant to tell her any of this. Now that she'd asked, she might as well know the whole story. At least if she heard it from him, he'd have a chance to tell his side.

"Kiat, but it wasn't —"

"I knew it!"

From the front room, Yshna called, "Sunnea, is anything the matter?"

"No, Papa, everything is fine." She glared at Elic. "Kiat? I knew it!" she whispered. "Why did you have to come and throw that in my face?"

"You asked!" Elic hissed back. "That's not what I came here to talk about. But it doesn't matter. She won't see me again."

"I can't imagine why not," Sunnea said with a haughty toss of her head. "You probably tried to kiss her or something."

"I did not! She kissed me!"

"Well, I never —!"

"I know. Goodbye, Sunnea. I have to get back to school."

Elic turned and walked away. Visiting her had been a mistake. He should have written her a note, the way he had when they were children. It would have given him a better chance of saying only the right things instead of stumbling into that trap about Kiat. In this mood, would she have read it? He hoped she would call him back, but she didn't say a word. So much for his dream.

Elic had no appetite for lunch, and no time to eat it, anyway. He didn't want to talk about the curse anymore. He gave the younger students a list of words to practice writing on their slates. He assigned the older girls a grammar exercise. While they worked, he watched, occasionally moving among them to help.

To Elic's relief, Kiat was not in school today. She was an ally, perhaps, but she'd kissed him. Seeing her in school was too awkward to imagine. He doubted she would try to remind him of it, but her presence would make it difficult to forget. And now Sunnea knew. The whole thing made his head hurt.

Brynnit looked up from her work and raised her hand.

"Do you have a question?" Elic asked.

With characteristic shyness, she looked down at the desk. "Teacher, are you angry?"

"No, of course not."

She met his gaze. "You've been frowning since we got here."

"Have I? I'm sorry, Brynnit." He tried to smile. "It has nothing to do with you. Go on with your lesson."

By the end of the school day, Elic's head was pounding. He trudged up to his mother's house for a remedy and walked in without knocking. Mam stood at the iron cookstove, preparing supper. Pap had made the stove for her. He had promised to make another for Elic and Sunnea. Elic didn't know whether he'd started it yet. The two cats, Ashy and Embers, lounged on a rug near the stove, Embers sprawled on her side, Ashy tucked up in a neat gray loaf.

Elic grunted a greeting. Mam turned with a smile. One look at him turned her expression to concern. "What's wrong?"

"Headache." He drew out a chair. He sat with his

arms folded on the table and rested his head on them.

Mam gave whatever she was cooking a good stir, then went to her store of medicinal herbs and selected something. Unlike Grammy Elika, she had no magic to aid her healing work but knew plant remedies for most common ailments. "I'll brew up some willow bark for you."

Elic mumbled his assent. It was a comfort to sit in the familiar kitchen and let her take care of him. She seemed glad to do it, even when he wasn't sick. When he first moved out, he had meant to fend for himself, but he let his mother do his laundry whenever she offered and ate her cooking three or four times a week. He knew men who wanted a wifc mainly to take over for their mothers — unfair to the wives, though he understood the desire. He remembered Kiat's wish to escape her mother. At least he'd never had reason to feel that way.

In winter, there was always a kettle of hot water on the back of the stove, ready to make tea or a medicinal brew. Mam poured some into a small pan and crumbled a pinch of willow bark into it. She stoked the fire under it to bring the water to a simmer.

"You don't feel sick otherwise? No fever, stomachache?"

"No. I've just been tense. Even Brynnit noticed."

"She's an observant child." Mam pushed his hair back to feel his forehead and fell silent. Finally, she looked him in the eye. "Where's your betrothal ring?"

"I took it out. It was bothering me." Elic wasn't in the habit of fibbing to his mother. The small lie was easier than the messy truth that he barely understood himself. He didn't have the energy to explain the whole sad story.

Telling it made it real.

"It doesn't look infected."

"No, that isn't the problem." He sighed. "It's Sunnea. We've been fighting."

"I wondered," she said. "What about?"

"It's not any one thing. Ever since the curse lifted, she's been different."

"Different?"

"We used to agree about everything. Now, she contradicts me and argues all the time. And I'm no better. I don't know what I want." He felt a warm rumbling weight on his lap. Ashy had settled there without his noticing until she began to purr. He stroked her soft fur.

Mam patted his shoulder. "These are strange days for all of us." She removed the pan from the heat and strained the brew into a cup. She set the steaming drink in front of Elic. He sipped. It was hot and bitter, but he trusted it would make him feel better. "You saw those men at the inn, making fools of themselves over Stell. When I woke up that morning, I was sure it must be the day we would leave for the city. Why else would I feel so excited?"

"What do you mean, we?"

"Stell and I. We were going to run off to Eukard City and have some sort of adventure."

"What did Grammy think of your plan?"

Mam chuckled. "I wouldn't call it a plan — more of a dream. We never got so far as to plan how we would go, or when, so I didn't tell her. I think she would have approved. She was on her own from an early age, and Stell and I assumed we could stay with my cousin

Balsam's family. Stoli would have been harder to convince. He didn't want to lose Stell's help. He didn't even want her to marry."

"So why didn't you go?"

"Your father started coming around." She smiled dreamily. "So we were married, and then you came along. Then Crane was born, and that's about when Yrae's Curse put an end to such dreams."

"Are you saying everyone feels as muddled as I do?"

"It must be hardest for you young folks. I can be nostalgic for the old days, before the curse. You're feeling all your dreams at once."

"What do you mean?"

"When you're young, you're supposed to have dreams and ambitions, plans and schemes. One day, you want one thing, the next, something else."

He nodded in recognition. "When we were boys, younger than Jagree, Crane and I had all kinds of plans."

"It's strange how Yrae's Curse didn't really affect children," Mam said. "Maybe he didn't think they were important. But when you were about twelve or thirteen, those dreams stopped, didn't they? Anything to do with leaving or doing anything different."

"Yes."

"I got to have my dreams when I was young and choose among them as I grew up. Your dreams got bottled up. You never got to change them, or refine them, or choose one over another. Until now. But how can you hope to choose the best one, if you have them all at once?"

Elic scratched Ashy behind the ears and under the chin. He didn't know whether it was the willow bark, the cat, or the conversation, but his headache was abating. "When Crane and I walked out of the curse," he recalled, "we almost couldn't stand, the freedom hit us so hard. We couldn't stop laughing for the longest time. And we remembered all our aspirations from when we were children. It didn't hurt like this. We had such a good time talking over those dreams."

"Maybe because you had someone to talk to. I've been watching. You're not the only one who feels this way."

He thought of Kiat, and the men at the inn that first night. It was true, other people had experienced odd reactions to the end of the curse. He hadn't imagined anyone felt it as drastically as he did. That could explain Sunnea's irritation.

"I expect it will settle down in time," Mam went on. "Like a fever, it has to run its course."

"Are you saying we're all ill?"

"Not now. But you were, in a way. We all were."

Elic nodded. He had felt ill after his return to Deep River. "So why aren't we better now?"

"Sometimes the recovery is the hardest part. Do you remember that winter your feet nearly froze?"

He shuddered at the memory. It was over ten years ago, but he could still feel the weight of those lifeless feet. Mam didn't even know the whole story. She thought he had just played in the snow too long with Crane. He'd never told her that after Crane went home, he'd gone to a pristine patch of snow behind Sunnea's house and stomped out, in letters as tall as himself, "I LUV YOU SOONEEUH." It took until sundown to finish, and the wind blew away his message in the night, misspelled name and all. Sunnea never saw it.

"I remember," he said. "I couldn't feel them. They were like blocks of wood."

"Until I warmed them up and the blood came back — how you howled! But without the pain, you would have lost your toes, or worse. That's where you are now. The blood's coming back. The dreams are."

Elic's head no longer throbbed, and he felt more hopeful. "Thank you. I'm lucky my mother is so wise."

She laughed and waved away the compliment. "Will you stay for supper?"

It was a tempting offer, but she'd done enough for him. "No, I want to be alone tonight. Thanks again, though. That really helped."

Elic returned home in a thoughtful mood. He hoped Mam was right, and his problem would pass in time. Then maybe he would know what to do. In the meantime, he picked up Soorhi's diary again while he ate his solitary supper of bacon and beans. He hoped Soorhi would write more about the Aklaka.

I traded a story for supper at the' inn in Misty Pass. I could have' traded my be'rrie's for a room, but I de'cided to sell the'm and sle'ep in the' stable'. If I'm going back to Eukard City, I will ne'ed a few duls in my pocket.

Elic was glad he now knew where Misty Pass was. But what did Soorhi mean, back to Eukard City? Elic read the line again to make sure he'd understood it. Although he was getting used to seeing Soorhi as a traveler, even an explorer, this idea was new and strange. While it made sense a footloose young man would likely end up in the capital city eventually, it was startling to have him write of going back there. When had he been there before?

> *It occurs to me' I neve'r set down the' cle'ar vision I had whe'n I trie'd liste'ning the' way the' Aklaka did. I will now, be'fore' I forge't. This vision was diffe're'nt, in that it didn't involve' the' pe'ople' I was with, at le'ast not dire'ctly. I saw a small valley I'm sure' I've' neve'r be'e'n to, though I would re'cognize' it if I saw it now. The're' was a whole' crowd of Aklaka, gathe're'd around a young man who looke'd like' Bushy, with Ersi's blue' eye's and the' be'ginnings of a be'ard. He' was the' smalle'st in the' group, though probably still quite' tall by our standards. They le'ft him all alone' the're'. Is this some'thing that has happe'ne'd alre'ady, or is it ye't to be'? And what doe's it have' to do with me'? But I thought, "Poor fellow."*

Elic's heart pounded as he closed the diary. The young man in the vision was like Jagree's description of the stranger at the Blue Heron, though younger. And Jagree's description had also sounded familiar at the time. Now Elic remembered — the dark blue eyes, from Soorhi's earlier description of his brother Ersi. But the man in the vision was not Ersi.

Elic went to bed still pondering the coincidence. He could understand how Soorhi might imagine a face that combined the features of his long-lost brother and his newfound friend. It didn't have to be a vision of a future event. But for Jagree to see a person who matched the description, in the flesh, in Deep River ... what did that mean?

As he drifted toward sleep, Elic lost the thread of this thought. With pleasure, he recalled the day when he and Crane approached and crossed the curse's boundary. Its power tried to turn them back. A strong enough will could overcome it. Crane pushed through, Elic followed, and they were free. It was a great day, even if they did have all their dreams at once. They hadn't tried to choose among them. All they did was celebrate.

When Elic returned alone, he had worried he might not be able to cross back over. Wasn't one effect of Yrae's Curse that no one came to Deep River? It seemed to apply only to outsiders. Elic crossed back with ease, only to feel the full weight of the curse on his soul. He hadn't been strong enough to escape it again on his own. He had known what it was, and what it meant to be free, but he couldn't experience that freedom or share what he'd known until the curse was lifted.

He dozed, warm and content. Now they were all free. Outsiders passed through nearly every day. Local people could leave if they chose. His dreams would sort themselves out, and he would know what he wanted. Maybe he already did know. He wouldn't be alone. He would have a family with Sunnea; the name Sulika was too pretty to waste. It would all turn out fine ...

He sat up abruptly, sleep chased away by a chilling thought. The stranger at the Heron — an outsider if ever there was one — had arrived before the curse was lifted. What kind of man could overcome a curse that kept even wizards away? Who was he?

Chapter 12. Stell's Old Friend

Elic woke early from troubled sleep and vague nightmares about wizards and curses. Only one person in Deep River could answer his questions about the stranger Jagree had seen. He went to the Blue Heron.

The rest of the village was just beginning to stir, but Stell was already up and busy when he arrived at the inn.

"Good morning, Elic. What brings you around so early?"

"I'm sorry to disturb you, Auntie Stell."

"Nonsense! We've barely spoken since you got over

your trouble. Breakfast?"

"I don't want to be a bother —"

"It's no bother. You look like you could use it. Sudi's right, you haven't been eating enough. You need a wife to fatten you up."

Elic didn't want to talk about marriage, so he followed Stell from the big common room into her kitchen. It was warm and filled with the delicious yeasty scent of bread dough, set to rise on a shelf near the brick oven. Elic sat at the table and let Stell serve him porridge and boiled eggs.

"That's right, you sit in Crane's spot." She sat across from him with her own breakfast. "Thank you for recommending Kiat, by the way. She's going to start tonight."

"I'm glad to hear it. She seemed ready for a change."

"Now, what's on your mind?"

"Did you know Soorhi kept a diary?" Elic thought it more likely he'd find answers if he edged into the question. "He left it for me, so I've been reading it. You wouldn't believe all the things he did — he met Mountain Folk once." He watched her for a reaction, but she only smiled and sipped her tea. "So, if you think it might be good story material, I could let you borrow it sometime."

"Thank you, that's very generous. You came over at this hour to tell me that?"

"You've had a lot of overnight guests lately," he said, changing tactics.

"It only seems like a lot because it's been so long. Winter's not the season for travelers. I didn't have any last night. That means we won't be disturbed." She gazed at him, waiting.

"So, there's no one here? Not even the stranger Ketty and Jagree brought down from the timber?"

Stell's eyes went wide, and she spurted a mouthful of tea back into her cup. "Did Jagree tell you that?" She set the cup down with a shaking hand. "Who else did he blab to?"

Elic hated to irritate her, but her reaction told him he was close to an answer. "I'm sure he hasn't told anyone else. I asked him about it because of something Crane said. About bringing his enemy here."

Stell gasped and stared at him. "Crane said that?" She took a deep breath before replying. "His enemy?"

Elic nodded but held his tongue. This was it, he was sure.

Stell sighed. "I guess he would — he was angry when he left here."

"So you were hiding someone! Is he still here?"

"No, he left before Crane did."

"I'm glad to hear that. I'm sure you meant well, but I didn't feel safe, knowing Crane's enemy might be in Deep River."

Stell was silent for a long time, intent on her breakfast. At last, she raised her gaze to Elic's. "My guest was not Crane's enemy," she said in a quiet, controlled voice. "He was ... an old friend."

"That's a relief. For all I knew, it was Yrae himself!"

Stell's smile didn't reach her eyes. "Yrae won't trouble Deep River again. Crane and my friend have seen to that."

"Are they greater wizards, then?" Elic asked. "Greater than Yrae?"

"Not greater. But better." Stell's smile was real now,

filled with confidence in the truth of her words.

"So your friend is a wizard, too. I wish I could have met him."

"He wasn't well most of the time. And he didn't feel at ease here."

Elic finished his breakfast and carried the dishes to the dishpan. "Was he used to finer places than Deep River?"

"He's strange around people, that's all. Very private."

"Oh." It reminded Elic of the description in the diary of Soorhi's father.

"But this is just between us," Stell said. "Even Jagree doesn't know this much, and you're not to tell him, or your mother, or even Sunnea. Promise?"

"Yes," Elic said. "I wanted to be sure we were safe from evil wizards."

"I can only speak for one."

Stell's assurance eased Elic's mind. He wished he could dispense with his personal issues as readily. He didn't know whether he wanted to reconcile with Sunnea because he'd dreamed of it or dreamed of it because he wanted it. Either way, Sunnea wasn't making it easy for him.

School kept him occupied all day. When it was over, he couldn't face his empty house. He ate a supper of beans and bacon again, more flavorful after sitting for a day. After the meal, Elic went out for a walk. The twilight was darkening rapidly, and the moon hid behind clouds. It was much darker than in his dream. He took a lantern.

He didn't have a destination in mind but found himself at the inn again. Outside, he met Kiat.

"On your way to work?" he asked. "Stell told me you'd accepted the job."

"I thought Ma would want to stop me, but she didn't even try. In fact, it was Pa who was against it at first. Ma told him I should see where this road leads. I'd never heard her talk that way before."

Elic remembered Ati's story about meeting Keena along the road after the curse was lifted. She had felt the change and let it change her. This was encouraging.

"Will you live at the inn, then?"

"I agreed to live at home for now, but maybe not for long."

He imagined Kiat leaving Deep River, and for a moment, envied her. "I've been thinking about what you said the other night. About Sunnea and me. Do you really believe we'll be together someday?"

"Can I see the future?" She furrowed her brow. "You were a nice pair who got along better than most. You shouldn't throw that away without a good reason."

"I agree, but I don't know how to get back to how we were. I tried to talk with Sunnea yesterday. It turned into an argument. Now she doesn't want to see me."

"Doesn't want to see you *yet*, you mean. How would you feel if she was pushing you to make a decision?"

"I know. It's hard to wait."

"It sounds like you know what you want."

Elic threw his hands into the air. "I'm not sure what I *know* anymore. Mam says we're having all our dreams at once, so none of us know what we want. But my ... my heart keeps following Sunnea."

"And yet here you are talking to me again." Kiat shook her head and smiled.

"That looks bad, doesn't it?"

"I'll help you any way I can, but spending a lot of time with another woman might send the wrong message." She winked. "I need to get to work, anyway."

She went inside. Elic considered going to call on Sunnea again, but every time things seemed hopeful, he was disappointed. It probably was better to wait. He turned around and went back home.

When he got there, he picked up Soorhi's diary to take his mind off his own worries. The new entry took up several days after the last one.

At last, I've reached Eukard City. I couldn't afford a seat on the coach, so I had to walk. As it was, I could only afford a room in the worst part of town. Still, it's good to be back. The buildings seem smaller, the trees look taller. But the last time I was in the city was the winter Ersi was born, so I must have been about 9. That means it's been 12 years! We always came to the city in the winter; most swamp people did. It was too cold to camp and there wasn't farm work. We'd get a cheap room and Pop would find whatever work he could, on the docks or in the markets. He said it was as easy to hide in a crowd as in the wilderness. He must have been right; I don't think anyone *e've'r bothe're'd us. He' was a country man at he'art — as soon as the' we'ather warme'd up, we'd go back to farm country. That's whe're' he' felt fre'e'. I think Mom would have' be'e'n happy to stay in the' city. I know I would have' be'e'n. So now's my chance'. I can hardly wait to start my ne'w life'.*

Elic closed the diary and got ready for bed. "That's how I feel, Soorhi. I can hardly wait to start my new life. I only wish I knew what it was."

Chapter 13. The River

During the night, a warm wind blew through Deep River. Elic woke more than once to the patter of melting icicles and the soft smash as they fell to the ground. In the morning, he looked out on slush and mud everywhere. The thaw made it feel like spring had come early.

Elic had forgotten to soak oats for breakfast, but after the success of his beans with bacon, he was determined to cook for himself more. He cut up the pork he'd gotten at the market and browned the meat in his big pot as he'd seen his mother do. He added water, and chopped up carrots, onions, and potatoes to stir in once it was hot. He ate cheese and an apple while waiting for the mixture to boil, then moved it to the side to simmer the rest of the day.

He slopped through the mud to the school and waited at the door to remind the boys to wipe their feet. If they weren't careful, this class could track in enough mud for a pig's wallow. Elic was willing to overlook a little dirt on a day like this. Hope surged in his heart. Kiat was right — Sunnea just needed time. He would give it to her, as much as she needed, but the outcome seemed assured. Like the weather, she would warm to him again.

"We need to talk more about Yrae's Curse," he announced as soon as the class was settled. If Mam was right, the older students would feel the breaking of the curse as much as he did, and no one was in a better position than Elic to warn them. "It kept our dreams in check, but now they've broken loose. We should expect a flood of new ideas." Lafa and Alryg laughed in agreement. "Some of these ideas might conflict with previous plans. They might be merely confusing, or they might seem crazy. Even dangerous."

"Give an example," Jagree called out.

"You, wanting to be an innkeeper," Elic retorted.

"An example that's not about me. Tell us one of yours."

Elic blurted the first thing that came to mind that wasn't about his problems with Sunnea. "Leaving Deep River."

The boys exchanged glances. "*You* wouldn't, though, would you, Teacher?" Rynk asked.

"I don't know," Elic answered honestly. "That one

seems to come up often. Maybe something less drastic." An idea popped into his head and out of his mouth — something he'd never considered before. "What if I wanted to run for mayor?"

Most of the class burst out laughing. All but Lafa. "That's not a bad idea, Teacher. Old Myn's been in office a long time."

"Thank you for your support," Elic said, startled anyone took his idea seriously. "The election is three years off, so I'll have plenty of time to decide. Which is the point I wanted to make — under the curse, I couldn't even *have* that idea. Having the idea doesn't mean I'm required to act on it. We're recovering from Yrae's Curse as if from a long illness. It may take some time to get back to normal. Or *normal* might be a different thing now."

The boys started swapping stories, and soon they were all talking and laughing at once. Elic allowed the cheerful disorder this time. From the sound of it, most of them had been troubled by startling new ideas. The ideas themselves weren't as troubling as the sense of being the only one. Elic read immense relief in every face. Their laughter reminded him of the day he escaped the curse with Crane. That was the right response, not silent suffering. They should enjoy their freedom.

When Elic went home for lunch, the house was fragrant with the simmering stew. He gave it a stir and threw in a handful of the kale. He fed the fire so it wouldn't go out. It was worth a cold lunch with that hot supper to look forward to.

He shared the same lesson about new ideas with the afternoon class. The younger children hadn't felt the curse directly and didn't know what he was talking about. "You're the lucky ones," he said, and gave them something else to work on while Farlyn, Alill, and Silib continued the discussion. They laughed as much as the older boys had; if anything, more loudly. Though they didn't talk over each other, the girls shouted their relief and excitement.

"It might be helpful to write about your experience," Elic suggested, thinking of Soorhi's diary. When they stopped talking and began to write, it was still not quiet. They had been talking over a steady background noise. It was a whisper and a roar, both familiar and strange.

Elic listened. He couldn't place the sound. Wind? But the wind had died down. Rain streaming off the roof? No, it was a dry day, and the sun was out.

Just then, Jagree burst in. He didn't bother to wipe his feet. "You have to see this." His eyes shone and a huge grin split his face. "All of you."

"What's so important?" Elic asked.

"There's water in the river."

"Of course there is, with all the snow melting. You interrupted my lesson and muddied my floor for a few puddles?"

Jagree shook his head impatiently. "Not puddles. Come and see." He dashed out.

The whole class turned to look at Elic. "Oh, all right." He led them outside and past his house to the riverbank, where Jagree waited.

"See?"

Muddy water raced down the channel that had been dry for as long as Elic could remember. It wasn't deep yet, but it wasn't puddles, either. Probably at least knee-deep already. It flowed swiftly, swirling around brush and boulders in the riverbed.

"The dam," Elic murmured.

"What did you say?" Jagree asked.

"Crane and I saw a mud dam that blocked the river and diverted it. It must have failed."

"Yes!" Jagree shouted. "That's where we found —"

Elic cut him off. "Found what?"

"You know," Jagree muttered. "That we brought to Stell."

Elic nodded. They couldn't discuss the stranger here, with the children close by, or even hint about him without provoking questions. And Elic had promised not to reveal what Stell had told him, even to Jagree. But it was curious that Stell's friend, a wizard, was found unconscious near the dam, at the edge of the curse's range. A curse that kept other wizards out.

Elic had always believed the loss of the river was part of the curse, until he saw the dam. It seemed too ordinary to be part of a magic spell. The river had dried up around the time the curse took effect. Now, the water had returned soon after the curse was lifted. And there was the dam's location, right at the curse's boundary. They must have been related, after all. Perhaps the stranger had something to do with it. If the curse couldn't keep him out, a mud dam could hardly stand against his power.

The flowing water proved a captivating sight for all ages. Liko scrambled into the branches of a misshapen old fruit tree for a better view. According to Soorhi, it was a sour cherry tree, though Elic had never known it to bear fruit.

"Careful!" he warned. "That branch could be dead, for all you know."

"It won't break," Liko insisted. "What's everybody pointing at?"

Elic followed his gaze upstream. Groups of villagers lined the riverbank, some watching the water while others pointed at something overhead. Elic couldn't make out what it was before a more immediate concern demanded his attention. Senri, Myn, and Foli leaned over the bank to drop dry leaves and blades of grass into the water. Close to the brink, they hopped and giggled as these improvised boats swirled away on the current.

"Who knows how to swim?" Elic asked. No child raised a hand. "Nor do I. Maybe next summer, we can learn. But that water looks too cold and swift. Don't fall in."

All the children backed up a step or two. Their eyes never left the rushing water. Elic looked upstream again at the humble stone houses, a few leafless trees, and sleeping kitchen gardens tucked under blankets of mulch for winter. The low winter sun glittered on the water and transformed the ordinary view into a pretty scene. All it took was a little water. The people along the bank laughed, the festive sound drifting on the breeze to his ears. Deep River wasn't a big, important town, but maybe it wasn't so bad. It had its place, on the bank of this river that was no longer dead.

And there was an even more captivating sight: in a vacant field near the inn, overlooking the river, Sunnea stood with a group of villagers, laughing and talking. Elic glanced at his students. It hardly seemed worthwhile to make them go back inside for an hour. Tomorrow was a rest day — they could start on it early. "Class is dismissed for the day," he announced. "Find your families and make the most of this historic occasion. You, too, Liko — out of the tree."

Liko scrambled down and joined the three younger boys in a resounding cheer before they ran off along the riverbank. Brynnit and Ylani joined hands and skipped away. The older girls smiled with delight at this unexpected freedom. As soon as they were out of sight, Elic hurried along the riverbank toward the inn, where he hoped to join Sunnea's group. His shortcut took him through a few back gardens. The road might have been a faster route, but no one else was on the road, either. All the interest was here, by the river. He passed little knots of his neighbors and picked up scraps of conversation.

"I'd forgotten what it was like," Kolma said with a dreamy smile. She was Liko's mother and Elic's nearest neighbor. "It looks right, doesn't it?"

"Did you see that eagle?" her husband Toli asked. "Why do you suppose it flew so low?"

"Fishing, I expect," Jelf said. Elic was surprised to see him outside the Village Hall before the end of the day, but this was no ordinary day.

"But it's too soon for fish!"

"A bird can hope, can't he?"

As Elic walked out of earshot, Jelf and Toli were recalling fish they had caught in their youth, the eagle forgotten for now. As he passed the back door of the Blue Heron, Stell came out with a large teapot, followed by Kiat carrying a tray of mugs. They moved from group to group, offering hot tea. Someone directed Stell's attention to the sky. Elic shaded his eyes and looked, too.

This time he spotted the silhouette of a large eagle circling low overhead.

As he walked past Stell, she chuckled. "I should have known."

Elic looked back at her. She continued to gaze at the eagle after everyone else returned to watching the river flow. He wasn't sure, but he thought she blew it a kiss. How strange. Hadn't Sunnea said something about seeing an eagle flying low the day the curse was lifted? Their first squabble before everything unraveled. Elic had been so sure he knew what she must have seen. What else had he been wrong about? He felt again her warm kiss on his cold cheek, the last kiss he'd had from her. He wished she would blow him one now.

Sunnea stood between the brothers Rovhi and Huvro, talking and laughing. Elic could hardly remember the last time he had seen her so animated. The mood suited her, bringing color to her cheeks and a sparkle to her eyes. Elic wished he were its cause, but it wasn't too late to join the group. Elic hadn't spent much time with either of the brothers since the days when they were all in school, but they were his friends, too. If he caught Sunnea in this happy mood, maybe she would agree to spend part of the free day with him, like the old days.

As he approached, she shook each brother's hand with undisguised warmth. "I'll see you at the dance in Bitter Springs, then." Huvro caught her by the waist and swung her around in an impromptu dance step. She twirled away from him, laughing. The brothers waved, a salute that included Elic, and departed.

Sunnea turned toward him as if she'd just noticed

him. Her laughter died away. "What do you want now?" Her frown matched his.

"I thought ... special occasion ..." He gestured at the people gathered nearby.

Kiat approached with her empty tray and slipped her arm through his. "I hear you're running for mayor."

Elic laughed. "Who told you that?" he asked. "It's just a crazy idea I had. Maybe it's something I was supposed to imagine a long time ago and be over by now."

Kiat waggled her head back and forth. "Maybe it's not such a crazy idea."

"Who would want a nineteen-year-old mayor?" Elic shook his head.

"You won't be nineteen by the time we hold an election," Kiat pointed out. "I'd vote for you." She winked, trailed her fingers down his arm, and walked away smiling.

Sunnea glared at him. "I don't believe it!"

"What?"

"After everything you said, you let Kiat flirt with you in front of me!"

"I didn't *let* her flirt with me. She did it all on her own. And what about you? You held hands with Rovhi and danced with Huvro right in front of me."

"In case you forgot, we're not betrothed anymore." She scowled. "And I wasn't *holding* hands. I was *shaking* hands. There's a difference."

"Hmph. So you'll see them at the dance, will you?"

"Everyone's going. Aren't you?" Sunnea asked.

Elic scowled. "I hadn't thought about it."

"Yet you're thinking of running for mayor, and that's years off."

"I am not. Forget about it." He turned and stalked away. There was no point in continuing the conversation when she was in such a thorny mood. Yet the idea of pulling her close and planting a kiss on her lips still stirred him.

"Psst!" someone hissed from the doorway of the inn.

Elic turned toward the sound. Kiat beckoned to him. "Did it work?"

"Sunnea's furious, if that's what you mean. What were you thinking?"

"I was thinking about last night — maybe you *do* want her to be jealous. Some people need a push."

"Please, don't help me that way. We'll sort it out for ourselves."

"Someday you'll thank me." Kiat grinned. "Sunnea won't be able to stop thinking about you now."

Elic sighed. "Thinking of terrible names to call me, no doubt." He turned back, hoping to explain. Sunnea was already gone.

People still gathered to watch the river run. The mild weather was a gift in itself, but they really had something to celebrate. For Elic, the novelty had already worn off. The return of the river no longer seemed like a hopeful sign. Maybe it wouldn't last. What would all their excitement mean if the river dried up again?

In a dark mood, he started to go home, with no plan for the rest of the day. Partway there, he changed his mind, cutting between the Village Hall and Jelf's house to a footpath that ran up the hill behind the town. At the top of the hill, a low stone wall surrounded the graveyard. A rose bramble clung to the wall, leafless and thorny. *Like Sunnea*, Elic thought sourly.

He passed through the gateway and walked among the graves. His grandparents Greelin and Elika lay side by side, their graves marked with low white stones, pieces knocked off the big white stone that served as Elika's doorstep. Soorhi's lay nearby, his stone marked with his dates and the words *Our Teacher*.

Elic knelt on the cold ground and rested his hand on the stone. "I found your diary. I don't know what most of it means. I don't know what any of *this* means." He waved a hand. "I wish you were here. You could always explain things better than anyone." Elic paused, listening. The wind carried the faint sound of rushing water. He smiled. "Crane broke Yrae's Curse. You were right about him. The river came back. I should be happy, but ..." Elic sighed and got to his feet. It would be dark soon. "I need to go. Thanks for listening, if that's something you can do."

Elic returned home to the savory smell of stew cooking, which cheered him some. To fill the time until supper, he picked up Soorhi's diary and turned to the next entry, which followed a gap of several weeks.

I have found work, which keeps me too busy for much writing. When I first arrived, I had an idea of working as a teacher, like Clover. But the only schools, as far as I can tell, are the Academy, which trains its own teachers, and the College, which deals in more advanced learning than I could hope to offer. The Academy educates the children of wealthy families, in separate schools for boys and girls. The' College' se'e'ms to be' only for young me'n, though pe'rhaps the're' is a 'Wome'n's College', too. A young maste'r at the' Acade'my share'd helpful information about a family se'e'king a private' tutor. So that's what I'm doing now: te'aching the' two sons of a rich te'xtile' me'rchant name'd Dubo. At first, I was e'xcite'd — he' has she'lve's of books in his study! But the'y are' all account books. The' boys are' e'ight and te'n ye'ars old, and ve'ry ... active'. Although no one' has said as much, I suspe'ct the' olde'r one' was e'xpe'lle'd from the' Acade'my. The'y are' spoile'd, ill-behave'd, and not e'age'r stude'nts. 'It is e'xhausting, but I do my be'st. This is not the' life' I e'xpe'cte'd in the' city. Pe'rhaps the' situation will be' te'mporary.

Elic chuckled to himself. Except for *spoiled*, the description of Soorhi's pupils could have applied to a boy named Elic. At least Soorhi had prior experience by the time he dealt with Deep River children. And he'd found the way to teach Elic, and all his friends. Most of them had come to enjoy school, at least a little. Dubo's sons didn't know how lucky they were.

Elic dished up a bowl of stew, blander and brothier than he had hoped, but hot and cooked through. As he ate, he turned to the next entry.

Strange' ne'ws! Dubo also has a daughte'r! He'r

name' is Dila. In the' month' I've' be'e'n he're', no one' saw fit to tell me'. We' me't today whe'n she' brought a me'ssage' to one' of he'r brothe'rs. She' is olde'r, thirte'e'n or fourte'e'n, and much brighte'r. She' se'e'me'd inte're'ste'd in the' le'sson, so I invite'd he'r to stay. She' was re'luctant, I thought be'cause' she' was starting in the' middle', but she' soon caught up. Late'r, I aske'd Dubo to le't he'r join us e've'ry day. He' re'fuse'd. She' le'arne'd the' basics as a child, and he' belie've's that is e'nough e'ducation for a girl who will marry in a fe'w ye'ars and be'come' a socie'ty matron. What would Clove'r say to that? It was all I could do to hold my tongue'. This isn't ove'r ye't.

Elic smiled to himself. He had known Soorhi only as an old man, an established authority figure. He enjoyed the image of Soorhi as a young rebel, not willing to take "no" for an answer.

As soon as he closed the diary, though, his thoughts turned back to Sunnea, going to the dance with someone else. Had she waited for Elic to invite her, and only accepted someone else when he failed? Or was this how she chose to use the time he was giving her? If she even knew he was giving it to her. He had followed Kiat's advice, not Sunnea's request. Every choice was going wrong, but Soorhi's words rang true: this wasn't over yet.

Chapter 14. The Waterfall

Elic drifted toward waking. It was a summer morning in the woods beside a murmuring river. Crane would continue his journey. Elic had to go back to Deep River for some reason ... a good reason ... Sunnea ...

He opened his eyes. It wasn't summer and there were no woods. He was home, Crane was long gone, and what of that good reason? It had failed to come true. At least he could hear the river. Its sibilant whisper found its way into all his dreams.

He rose and dressed in his chore clothes, though he

had no plans for the day. He'd lost the chance of spending it with Sunnea. He wasn't sure he even wanted to see her now. What good was it when he always said the wrong thing? She insisted on asking questions, then objected to his truthful answers. He wasn't about to lie to her. Avoiding her was easier.

Elic would be alone, after all. There would be no little girl named Sulika. Even if, by some miracle, he had a family with another woman, their names would join differently. He spent a moment mourning a child who did not, and would not, exist. With a sigh, he put two eggs on to boil and picked up Soorhi's diary to pass the time.

I spent my day off as usual, exploring the' city, but today was a little' diffe'rent — Dila came' with me'. She's be'en "happe'ning by" the' schoolroom re'gularly and joining le'ssons in se'cret. He'r brothe'rs don't se'em to care', and she's a fine' stude'nt. I wish we' didn't have' to sne'ak. I thought he'r fathe'r might disapprove' if she' came' with me' out into the' city. I'm a grown man of 21; at 14, she's still a child, though it isn't difficult to picture' the' woman she' will be' in a fe'w ye'ars. Not to me'ntion the' class diffe're'nce' of me' be'ing in Dubo's e'mploy. Dila explaine'd she' was going to visit he'r uncle'. Could she' help it if I tagge'd along part of the' way? She' is a cle've'r girl and knows he'r own mind! Whe're' doe's she' ge't it? I was e'age'r to me'et he'r uncle' until she' explaine'd he' was re'ally he'r mothe'r's uncle'. I've' me't he'r mothe'r Lily only twice'. She's in poor he'alth and rare'ly le'ave's he'r room or doe's anything. I gue'sse'd the' uncle' would be' more' of the' same', only olde'r. Imagine' my surprise' whe'n Dila marche'd up to the' Wizards' Hall and aske'd for Uncle' Dillum! He' is an olde'r man, but vigorous. I could te'll just by looking he' was a powe'rful wizard. This is Dila's kin? Now she' make's more' se'nse'. She's not magic folk he'rse'lf, but she' has the' same' curiosity and inte'llige'nce' as he'r uncle'. And he' adore's he'r. He' was also kind to me'. I think he' misunde'rstood why I was the're', though, as if I might be' a wizard myse'lf. I had ne've'r be'e'n to the' Wizards' Hall be'fore', so I was curious and aske'd que'stions. Was it a school? Not formally, but like'ly candidate's can come' the're' to find a te'ache'r. It se'e'ms to be' more' of a social hall whe're' wizards can me'e't, share' a me'al, and le'arn ne'w tricks. Dillum said I was we'lcome' anytime' — they're' always glad to se'e' "my kind." I trie'd to e'xplain my position in Dubo's house'hold, that I'm just a te'ache'r. I'm not sure' he' he'ard ...

Elic slapped the diary down on the table. He was too restless to read. He peeled and ate the eggs with bread, in too much of a hurry to even make tea. Between dreaming about Crane and reading of Soorhi exploring the city and meeting a wizard, he felt compelled to go *out*, no matter where.

He put on his coat and pulled open the side door. It resisted but opened more easily than before. It was another sunny day — almost warm, at least for early winter. The river called. He walked to the bank and gazed at the swift water. It looked deeper since the previous day, though shallow compared to its old channel. He pictured creeks and rain feeding it. How deep might it get?

"Crane, I wish you could see this," he whispered. "You're missing everything."

While it felt good to be outside, he didn't have anything to do. He was tempted to work in his vegetable garden. The soil was too wet for digging and it was the wrong season to plant flowers or vegetables, but mulch would keep down weeds and hold the moisture for when it was needed. He was about to go ask Jagree for some straw when his brother squelched up the muddy path past the school.

"Hey, Jagree," Elic said. "I was on my way to see you about —"

"Can it wait? I thought you might want to come with me." Behind Jagree, a mule stood patiently waiting.

"Come with you where?"

"Don't you want to see what happened to the dam? Pap let me borrow Rabbitears."

"I noticed. You forgot to tie him."

Jagree glanced at the mule with a grin. "I didn't forget. Are you coming?"

Elic sighed. "Fine, why not?" It was better than

nothing, and maybe they'd learn something useful.

Jagree splashed back to the standing mule and sprang onto its bare back. Although not wearing his good clothes, Elic picked his way more gingerly, avoiding the worst of the mud, and scrambled up behind Jagree. "No saddle?"

"Rabbitears doesn't like it. Grip with your knees and you'll be all right."

They started off at a gentle walk. Even at the slow pace, Elic was sure he would slide off, but as he grew accustomed to the rocking motion, he moved with the animal and felt more stable. It was a long time since he'd ridden anything. He rarely had a reason to go anywhere he couldn't walk. Maybe that would change now. He could go anywhere, like ... like ... anywhere. Elic had never been interested in horses and riding the way Jagree was. Elic had a vague memory of sitting on a pony with Crane, when they were small boys. Crane fell off as soon as the pony took a step, Elic recalled with a nostalgic smile. Back when Crane couldn't do anything right. How things changed.

The Mountain loomed ahead of them, shining white against the pale blue sky. The air was so clear, the distant peak looked close enough to climb before lunch. The dark smudge Elic had seen earlier was hidden by fresh snow.

Jagree chuckled.

"What's funny?" Elic asked.

"You say you've been thinking about leaving, but this is the first trip either of us has taken since the curse was lifted."

"You're right, it is kind of absurd." Elic's spirits lifted.

Maybe this was just what he needed.

Outside town, the road bent north, but Rabbitears plodded southwest into open fields and brushland. There was no path except a faint track where the dead grass had been trodden down.

"Listen to that," Jagree said.

"What?"

"The river. Everything's different, isn't it?"

"Some things are."

They rode on in silence, accompanied by the river's whisper. The noise, constant but gentle, soothed Elic. This outing was an excellent idea.

"How's Sunnea these days?" Jagree asked.

"She's ... fine," Elic replied, tense again.

"I think she worried almost as much as Mam when you were ... whatever it was you were. She was always coming over to help Mam bring you food. Now we don't see her much."

"I'm better now." Elic wanted to change the subject as soon as possible. He noticed the mule lacked not only a saddle but also bit and bridle. "How do you direct him without reins?"

"I just tell him where to go." Jagree spoke as if it were obvious.

"You tell him."

"Sure. He's got big ears, so it's no problem."

"What if he decides not to listen to you?"

"Then we go where he wants. Mostly, he listens to me. Shall we go a little faster?"

Before Elic could answer, the mule broke into a quick trot. Mud flew from his hooves and spattered Elic as he clung to Jagree and adjusted to this new motion. It was too late to change his mind. At least it was better than fighting with Sunnea.

Rabbitears slowed when they reached the pine woods. The river's whisper grew to a roar as they picked their way through the trees.

"This is about where we found that stranger," Jagree said. "The dam was over there."

"I know." Elic slid off the mule, wincing. His legs were cramped and sore, but he didn't complain aloud. Jagree jumped down with no sign of discomfort.

Elic walked stiffly to the top of the slope. When he had hiked it last, with Crane, he had been bent under the weight of Yrae's Curse. At least he didn't have to fight that burden now. Where the dam of mud and debris had been, water poured over a rock shelf in a small, noisy waterfall. Some mud and sticks clung to the banks on both sides, but the dam was gone. Across the river, a rocky ridge jutted from the hillside and fell away to the east in gentle, aspen-clad slopes. The river split around this ridge, most of the water following the south fork. But a significant amount tumbled down the waterfall to its old bed, now the north fork. While it was unlikely to fill the channel to its old depth, it did not appear the river would dry up again anytime soon.

"This is where Crane and I crossed out of the curse."

"Did Crane do this?" Jagree pointed to the waterfall.

"I don't know," Elic said. "He's been gone awhile — how long, a week? — and the water is just now coming back."

"Maybe it needed time."

Elic nodded. That could be true, just as it was taking time to shake off all the effects of the curse. He thought again of Stell's mysterious friend. Crane wasn't the only wizard who had passed through recently. Although it might not have been magic at all. Maybe the dam had simply weakened and failed after so many years.

"Or maybe it was the flood that did it," Jagree said, continuing his own thought, not responding to Elic's unspoken musings.

Elic glanced at him, startled. "What flood?"

"When Ketty brought me here, the river was a lot higher than this, full of trees and mud. Boulders, too."

"Trees and boulders? Where did they come from?"

"Where does the river come from?"

Elic followed his gaze to the looming Mountain, visible through the sparse woods. So the eruption had done damage, though not where Elic could see it. He recalled his vision on the night of his walk with Kiat — the valley as a vast river bursting out of the Mountain — and shuddered at the thought of that grinding flood reaching the village.

"We had to shout to be heard over it," Jagree continued. "I couldn't believe the dam would hold against that, though it seemed untouched at the time. It's strange it should break now."

"The flood probably weakened it," Elic said. "We were lucky it held as long as it did." Perhaps the dam that had robbed them of irrigation water for eighteen years had saved them in the end. "How did Ketty know to come here? Did she and Crane travel this way?"

"She didn't tell me. I don't think they traveled together. Anyway, they didn't arrive together. Crane and the stranger might have come this way, though. Ketty had a horse, so she must have come by the road from

Misty Pass. But she knew right where to look for the old man, as if someone had told her."

Elic gazed at the surrounding woods, through which he had hiked with Crane on a summer day that seemed long ago. This was gentle country, especially on a mild day. But it grew more rugged the farther into the hills one ventured. On his brief journey, the only paths he encountered were made by animals, and he hadn't seen any person except Crane. It would be a hard trek in winter. Why risk it? And why, after reaching shelter and safety in Deep River, had the stranger returned here? Or had Crane left his companion in the woods and gone to get help? According to Stell, they had both been ill. If that were the case, how had Crane made it all the way to Deep River, on foot? It was possible they weren't traveling together, though that would mean the stranger was following Crane — or pursuing him.

"Who do you think he was?" Elic asked. He couldn't reveal what Stell had told him about the stranger, but Jagree had seen the man with his own eyes and helped bring him to the inn. Maybe he could shed some light on why he was out here alone.

Jagree laughed. "With that wild beard? Wizard, of course."

Elic stared. Had Jagree figured it out for himself? Stell hadn't told him. Elic recalled Soorhi's first impression of the wizard Dillum. Was it that easy to tell on sight?

Jagree laughed harder. "I'm joking with you. How would I know who he was? But Ketty — I *know* she's magic. That's probably how she knew where to find him."

Jagree continued to smile as he stared into the distance. He no longer looked mischievous. Elic had never seen such an expression on his brother's face, but he knew what it meant — the boy was smitten. Ketty must be quite a woman. Unfortunately for Jagree, she seemed to be involved with Crane. There was a change — Crane had a sweetheart at last, just as Elic had lost his. Elic pushed away the low mood that threatened whenever he remembered that loss. It was too beautiful a day to sustain more than a prick of envy.

"This is a pretty spot now," Elic said. "Too bad we didn't bring something to eat."

Jagree shook himself out of his trance. "Are you kidding? It's too cold for picnics. Come on, if we hurry, maybe Mam will feed us both."

Elic hated to leave the sun-dappled woods and splashing waterfall. He felt closer to the absent Crane here, and to his own brief adventure. But hot food in his mother's kitchen was a tempting lure. Jagree hopped with ease onto Rabbitears' back. With a groan he couldn't suppress, Elic dragged himself up behind.

"Could we take it easy going back?" he asked.

Jagree chuckled at the request but maintained a gentle pace. They descended out of the sparse woods and crossed a pasture. The sun, as high as it would get on this winter day, cast their shadows onto brown, sodden grass. A cold breeze carried away any heat the sun might have lent them.

"That fellow might have been a ... what do you call 'em? From the mountains?" Jagree commented.

"What, Mountain Folk?" The hair prickled on the back of Elic's neck.

"No, they're supposed to be giants, aren't they? He wasn't *that* big." Jagree leaned forward as if to consult with the mule. He straightened again. "Hermits, that's the word."

"What do you know about hermits?"

"Not much," Jagree admitted. "I remember Soorhi said something once. They're supposed to be hard to find but worth talking to. Wise or something. I always imagined they'd have big beards."

Elic laughed. "I suppose they would. What would a hermit be doing way down here?"

"I don't know. Maybe he wanted to taste Stell's cooking?"

Elic forced a smile. Jagree didn't know how close he was to the truth. "I don't remember Soorhi mentioning hermits," he said, to steer the conversation back to safer ground.

"It was a long time ago, when I was still in the baby class."

"Don't call it that." No matter how Elic stressed the equality of both classes, many of the boys regarded the morning class as better somehow. Because they didn't have to share with beginners? Because they got to move to a new class? Maybe it really wasn't as fair as Elic had thought.

"Fine, when I was in the *afternoon* class, then. Maybe he didn't tell you big fellows."

"Did you know he met hermits?" Elic said. "When he wasn't much older than you?"

Jagree turned to gape. "No! Really?" He frowned. "But if he never mentioned them to you ..."

"I found his diary," Elic replied, pleased he'd

successfully diverted Jagree from the mysterious stranger. It wasn't Elic's place to spread Stell's secrets, though she had barely told him anything. "I've been reading it. He led an interesting life."

"Are we talking about the same Soorhi? He was just a teacher."

Elic frowned. Soorhi had said the same thing about himself. Elic didn't want to accept the dismissive phrase from either of them. "We only knew him as an old man. He did all kinds of things before he came here — collected stories from hermits, lived in the city, met Mountain Folk —"

"Met Mountain Folk?!" Jagree squeaked. "They're real? Are they really giants? What did they look like?"

"It was ... hard to tell from his written description." Without meaning to, Elic had brought the conversation back to the stranger, who fit Soorhi's description almost exactly. "But I don't think they were giants, just very tall."

"Oh." Jagree sounded disappointed, though he soon brightened again. "Are they still there?"

"I don't know. Soorhi wrote about meeting them seventy years ago. A lot can happen in that time. But he said they were good at hiding."

Jagree sighed. "All the adventures happen to somebody else."

"You're young. Who knows what you might do?"

Jagree nodded as he considered this. "Maybe I'll meet Mountain Folk one day."

Elic chuckled. "Sure." *Maybe you already have*, he added to himself.

Chapter 15. The Next Mayor

As Elic and Jagree returned to the village, they passed Old Myn's house. The mayor sat on his porch with two of his cronies, Raffyn and Tikum. Raffyn had left his farm to his son and now lived with his daughter's family in the village. That meant six in the miller's house, but it was bigger than the little farmhouse, especially now that Breff and Tiek had their twins. Tikum lived with his son's family next door to Elic and helped with the cobbling work. Mostly, these older men spent their afternoons gossiping on somebody's porch and evenings playing dice at the Blue Heron. They'd worked hard all their lives; they had earned it.

"Good afternoon!" Elic greeted them.

Raffyn and Tikum smiled and waved. Old Myn glowered. "Behold our next mayor, covered in mud and riding on a mule," he spat. "A muddy pup!"

Elic's face burned as the men's laughter followed him. He must look ridiculous. And it seemed his offhand comment about running for mayor had turned into full-blown news overnight. The way rumors spread, the whole town must know by now. It didn't matter that Elic himself didn't take the idea seriously.

"I'll be glad when that blows over," he muttered. "I wonder who told him."

"Does it matter?" Jagree asked. "It's a great joke. About time someone upset that mule-headed old windbag!" He patted Rabbitears' neck. "No offense."

The mule responded with a whicker Elic could have sworn sounded amused.

Mayor Myn had been elected a year or so before Yrae's Curse, and re-elected every time for twenty years, as if no one could think to do things differently. Under the curse, they probably couldn't. He acted like he had the job for life and puffed it up with more importance than it deserved. The mayor's chief duties entailed presiding over the occasional town meeting, casting the deciding vote in case of a tie, and ensuring cooperation with the tax gatherer. Old Myn relished the respect his position brought him, even if it was mostly ceremonial. Elic agreed with Jagree; there was some satisfaction in annoying the pompous old fellow.

They returned the mule to the shed, a structure just

big enough for Pap's wagon and stalls for Rabbitears and a cow. There wasn't room for Jagree to keep a horse of his own. At least he had horses to care for at the Blue Heron.

The brothers washed at the pump behind the house, then went in for lunch, a hearty soup of chicken and vegetables with thick noodles.

"What an honor!" Pap cried as they came into the house. "Mayor Elic!"

"Ohme, don't tease," Mam said. "It's silly gossip."

"You won't think it's silly when it comes true," Pap said.

"As my first act, I forbid further mention of this topic," Elic said.

"Yes, Your Honor," Jagree replied with a solemn expression and a deep bow. Even Elic had to laugh, along with his parents, but after that, they complied with his request. They also avoided mentioning Sunnea, though his mother bit her lip more than once during the meal.

"It's a good thing you boys got out and enjoyed the day," Pap said. "This mild weather won't last. I predict another hard freeze before the big dance next week, and then we'll probably be snowed under for the rest of the season."

The dance. That was another topic Elic wished to avoid. He changed the subject. "I guess I'd better get that straw on my garden today."

"We can get it now, if you're finished," Jagree said.

"Do you want some of this soup to take home?" Mam asked. "I made too much for us to finish." Without waiting for his response, she began ladling it into another large pot.

"I won't be able to eat that much!" Elic protested. "Won't it spoil?"

"Keep it on your porch. This time of year, it'll stay fresh there. Put a rock on the lid to keep pests out, and it should be fine."

"Thank you. I'll come back for it later."

The brothers crossed the road and went around the back of the stable, where Jagree piled the dirty straw from the stalls. "How much?"

"One load should do it," Elic replied. "Lend me your barrow?"

"Technically, it's Stell's barrow. Maybe someday, though, when this is mine ..." Jagree gazed at the back wall of the stable with longing, as if he saw more than a stone wall, a stable. He seemed to be over his idea of working for Stell and had moved on to an idea of working for himself.

"We'll take it from the middle, where it's hot, so you don't get as many weed seeds." Jagree forked straw from the pile. It steamed in the chilly air.

Elic returned home with the barrow full of the reeking, half-rotted mixture of straw and manure. He was glad he didn't have to pass Old Myn's house again. As he spread it over his garden plot, he imagined the rich, moist soil of spring. Most of his gardening knowledge came from Soorhi, who had worked this plot before him. From him, Elic had learned what to plant and when, how to save seeds, how to feed the soil as well as himself. There was no shame in being dirty if you made something grow.

By the time he finished, Elic was beyond dirty and in

a good mood again. There was Mam's soup, but he would need a bath before he went anywhere. He was only a little surprised when he found the soup pot already on his porch, with a large rock holding the lid down. Mam wouldn't admit she spoiled him, but she did. Elic smiled and drew enough water for a bath. While it heated, he opened Soorhi's diary to the next entry.

Bad news — I've lost my position, and in the middle of winter, too. I thought Dila was being discreet, but somehow Dubo found out she was sharing her brothers' lessons. He wasn't happy and he wouldn't listen to reason. I tried to explain that nothing improper was going on between us, but this only made him more upset. I cannot believe that a loving father would rather his daughter be kept in ignorance than risk the slight scandal of being taught by a man! So now I'm starting over again. Good thing I saved most of my pay. If I'm careful, I can live for months, if necessary. I've got a room in a part of town that seems familiar — I think Mom and Pop must have lived here in winters when I was a child. I feel right at home. But I miss Dila.

It was hard for Elic to imagine someone who thought boys should be schooled but not girls. He didn't separate his classes because girls lacked ability. On the contrary, they were often his best students Elic would never tell either sex they couldn't or shouldn't learn. Soorhi had separated the classes from the start, and Elic continued the arrangement. It had more to do with distraction: teasing, flirting, disappearing into a shell of shyness and embarrassment. It was easier not to deal with these behaviors in the classroom.

But was it fair that only the girls had to share a classroom with the young beginners? Elic had never considered organizing things differently. Soorhi's way was the only way he knew. The curse probably hadn't helped. Elic tried to ensure each student received instruction suited to their age, ability, and experience. With both beginners and more advanced students in the same classroom, though, his attention was pulled in more directions. He couldn't count on always having a helper, and anyway, he was the teacher. There wasn't space in the classroom for everyone at once. There wasn't enough of Elic to teach three separate classes. If he put the little boys into the morning class, would the older boys rise to the occasion and be good examples, or would they teach the young ones to misbehave? Would they all assume they were superior? If he put the little girls with the older girls, would they assume they were so different from boys that they had to be separated? Maybe it would be better to give the beginners their own class and put all the advanced students in one class, distractions or not.

Once the kettle boiled, Elic poured cold water into the tub and added boiling water until it reached a comfortable warmth. He undressed and hung his dirty clothes near the fire to dry. That would make it easier to knock the mud off before washing them. It would still be a job, but one he wouldn't foist onto his mother this time. He climbed into the bath and scrubbed off the grime. Bathing before supper was one of the few advantages of living alone. In his mother's house — probably all mothers' houses — the weekly bath took place after the dishes were done, before bedtime.

Elic lathered and rinsed his hair. He was glad he didn't have to use someone else's bath water or share with a younger brother. He would be willing to share with Sunnea, though. Not that both of them would fit in this tub. He imagined her in the bath, and himself washing her. He would be happy to use rose-scented soap in that situation. It was such a compelling image, he could hardly believe he'd never thought of it, even under the curse. He could almost feel her bare, wet skin …

It was a pleasant daydream, though he felt a little ashamed. He'd never entertained such notions, even when he planned to marry her. Surely she didn't imagine him in her bath! It was harmless and she would never know, but still … He splashed out of the cooling water to dry off in front of the fire.

He put on clean clothes and considered supper. He could heat some of the soup, though he didn't have the energy to even go to that much trouble — he was tired and sore from the long ride and the garden work. But if he walked over to the Heron, he would be rewarded with hot food, already made, and agreeable company. He retrieved his money bag from his dirty trousers and peered at the coins. He'd spent little since buying the silver pin — eight duls wasted. There was more than enough for a supper at the inn.

It was dark by the time Elic stepped outside. A thin glaze of ice covered the mud in the path. It crackled, then gave underfoot, frozen only at the surface. Cold as the night was, it would be solid ice by morning. The clear sky glittered with stars, except for a patch in the north where a cloud blotted out their light.

The Blue Heron was bright and warm by contrast. Stell came out of the kitchen as Elic entered. "Elic, good evening! Supper tonight, or just ale?"

"Supper *and* ale." He looked around for an empty seat. The place was busy, but he spotted an unoccupied chair at one of the long tables — across from Old Myn. The mayor frowned at Elic as he approached.

"Sir," Elic said, and made a small bow. Old Myn was only a year or two older than Elic's father but had been called Old Myn at least since he was first elected mayor. It was almost a title. Elic had never liked him, but he deserved the same respect as any grown person in town.

"Pup," Myn growled.

Elic smiled with as much mild humor as he could manage. "I don't know what you've heard. I want you to know I meant nothing against you."

"I see. You want to take my job, but it's nothing against me. Thank you very much."

"I'm not sure I do." With effort, Elic kept his voice level. "It was an example, for the benefit of some curious boys, of an unusual idea. We'd been talking about Yrae's Curse, and the changes since it was lifted, and —"

"You say there was a curse before. I say we're under a spell now! Soon, no one will remember how to behave decently anymore." Old Myn gazed past Elic at one of the tables by the window. Elic didn't know whether Myn meant the strangers seated there, or Kiat serving them. "Strangers in town, dances ... I don't like it."

"I'm sorry," Elic said.

"It's not your fault, but I accept your apology."

Elic remembered their earlier conversation at this table. "You wondered once when things would go back to the way they were before the curse was lifted. What if they go back to how they were before the curse?"

"I don't want to think about it! People could leave and not come back." Old Myn scowled. "See how you like it when your wife leaves you."

Elic sat back with a start. While he didn't have a wife yet, and Sunnea hadn't exactly left him, the comment was close to the mark. "But your wife didn't leave," he said, as tactfully as he could. "She died, only five years ago, wasn't it? Still under the curse."

Myn shook his head. "Farni was my second wife, who I married to give Mynna a mother. I do not speak my first wife's name, since she went to visit her sister in Oxbow and never came back."

This was all news to Elic. It had happened when he was too young to know about it; no one discussed such scandals in front of children, anyway. Maybe that was why Myn was so difficult. "I ... I'm sorry."

Myn gave a gruff nod. He stood, left a few coins on the table, and departed.

Stell swept over and placed a bowl of thick ham and bean soup and a plate of fresh bread in front of Elic. Kiat followed with a mug of ale.

"Brave of you, talking to Myn," Stell said as she scooped up the coins. "He's been in a foul mood ever since the enchantment was lifted. Worse than usual, I mean."

"He was telling me about his first wife. Did she really leave him?"

She stopped what she was doing and stared at him. "He spoke her name?"

"No. So it's true?"

"She left him as soon as Mynna was weaned," Stell said. "There was talk that she ran off with some man. I wouldn't be surprised if she just up and left on her own. I can't say I blame her."

"You mean Myn was always this way, even before?"

"As long as I've known him. I suppose it didn't help when Halla left, but some people can't stand any change."

She bustled off to serve another guest. It explained a lot about Old Myn's irritation in general, and especially toward Elic. Based on Ati's comments at the betrothal supper about her kinfolks' odd behavior, Elic assumed she felt the same way about the changes in Deep River. Elic didn't know what her reasons were. She would probably be as pleased as Elic when Sunnea came to her senses and started acting like her old self again. If she ever did.

Myn's seat did not remain empty for long. Kiat's father, Briato, soon took his place. He had eaten at home but lifted a cup for an appreciative sip of ale. "Interesting times, eh?"

"You could say that. How, for you?"

"A fellow came up from Sage Valley today — that's south, across the ford. He grows flax down there and thought there might be a market up here. I took one look at his yarn and bought everything he had. Beautiful!"

"That's nice," Elic said, though he had little interest in the subject.

"Yshna will be glad. He's very particular about the material for Sunnea's new dress and hasn't been happy with anything I've shown him. But I think he'll be pleased with a nice linen. Maybe cream, with blue stripes."

Elic had to agree Sunnea would look lovely in that. She looked lovely in anything. Or nothing.

Before he could dwell on that thought, Stell interrupted. "How about a story?"

The crowd responded immediately by gathering around her seat by the fire. Elic joined them. Most of the tales were familiar. She ended with one he didn't recall hearing before.

"This is one I learned from Soorhi. I haven't told it in a long time, but I remembered it today." She smiled at Elic, and he guessed she had read the story in Soorhi's notes. It was a strange one, about people turned into animals and plants by magic. Some of them longed to be human again and rejoiced upon being set free. Others forgot they were human and lived happily as trees and deer and rabbits, but when released, slowly recalled their old lives and returned to them. All except one, who remained stubbornly in the forest, believing himself a tree until the day he died.

"And then he thought he was a log," Stell concluded.

The crowd was silent a moment, before breaking into appreciative laughter. Elic suspected she had made up that ending herself, in honor of Old Myn. She had a gift for twisting even familiar tales in unexpected directions.

As the other guests headed for the door, Elic helped Kiat collect dirty cups and put them in the dishpan, as he had often helped Crane.

"You don't have to do that," Stell said.

"I want to help. You've cheered me up tonight."

"Thank you, then. You and your brother are alike, always making yourselves useful. He'll make someone a fine husband one day."

"Jagree?" Elic laughed. "If you say so."

"I do say so. And so will you."

Behind her, Kiat smiled. "I couldn't have said it better."

"I hope you're right," Elic said. "Good night, and thanks again for the stories."

He returned home, warm and happy from his evening out. Maybe things were improving. At least he wasn't a tree.

It had been good practice, apologizing to Old Myn, being contrite and respectful even when he hadn't done anything wrong. Before he fell asleep, Elic lay in the dark and planned what he would say to Sunnea the next time he saw her, a speech full of apologies and compliments and proper, respectful comments. Even Ati would approve. Once again, he slept with the voice of the river in his ears. Perhaps that was why he dreamed of Sunnea stepping out of a tub, warm and dripping, and into his arms.

Chapter 16. Ice

A loud thump woke Elic. He listened in the dark as the wind whistled around the house and rattled the door. Pap was right about the change in the weather. It was freezing in the house — the fire had gone out.

Another gust thumped the door. Not likely he'd get back to sleep, so Elic shivered out of bed and fumbled in the dark to light the lamp. He kindled a new fire, then crawled back under the covers with Soorhi's diary to wait for the house to warm up.

It's been a long journey, but I've found the life I was meant to live. It seems so obvious now; would I have found it without everything else I've endured? I've been talking to people in this poor part of town and determined there is a need and a desire for Clover's kind of school, where any child can come and get a basic education. With some of my savings, I rented a vacant store building with space for a classroom in front and small living quarters behind. I've been busy getting ready so haven't had a chance to write here in weeks. I had to build benches and desks myself — I'm not much of a carpenter, but I gained a few skills in Appleseed. As always, I find something else from that time for which to be grateful. Today was the first day of school. I wasn't sure how many students to expect, but had twelve, ranging in age from 5 to 13. None have had any formal schooling. A few have picked up a little at home. I charge a small tuition to those who can afford it, but most can't. I would like it to be a truly free school. I don't know how that will be possible. I have to live, too.

Elic looked up from the book and watched the fire burn. He had never needed to worry about how he would live. The townsfolk taxed themselves to pay his salary, an arrangement established back in Soorhi's day. Elic could offer an education to any child, without concern for his own pay. It was strange to imagine Soorhi struggling at anything, and at the same time, intriguing to see him at the beginning of his career. In that far-off city, making up every step as he went along, he planted the seeds that bore fruit in Deep River.

Elic read on, an entry from a few weeks later.

I never knew I could be this tired. I feel like I have been on my feet without a rest for days! But the Free School is a reality. Although I didn't have steady attendance at first, now I have a class of fourteen — six boys and eight girls. Ordy, one of the boys in the class, keeps us entertained. He's no more than 8, and he has learned some amazing tricks. One day, he walked on his hands up the middle of the classroom — probably six steps — when he thought I couldn't see. Of course, I could see him, the way I do when my back is turned. I congratulated him on his talent but asked him to save it for after school. He said, "Teacher, you have eyes in the back of your head!" That same day, a woman came to the school after class, much better dressed than we normally see down here. She was very interested and offered to "subscribe." I revealed my ignorance, and she explained she approved of my effort and wanted to give money to support the school! And she knew others who would do the same if I came and spoke to them. I have been out every night in my best clothes, trying to talk money out of rich people. It's much harder work than teaching! Some give, some don't, but the school is well taken care of now. Women seem especially interested, which intrigues me. These are women of Dubo's class, yet I can't imagine him supporting a school like mine. Were these women educated? Are their daughters? I am heartened to think Dubo represents only himself.

The house was warm now, and Elic wanted breakfast. He closed the diary and got out of bed, awed at the effort Soorhi had put into funding his first school. He appreciated his own position more than ever.

When he opened the door to go to school, an icy wind carried a dusting of white into the house. Powder snow had drifted knee-deep on the porch overnight. Elic grabbed the broom and scattered the snow out of his path. No more snow fell, and in places, the wind had swept the ground bare as neatly as his broom. Drifts lay against houses and fences.

He arrived at school to find Yrae's Curse had been replaced as the topic of greatest interest. The river was beginning to freeze. The boys had seen snow, frost, and frozen puddles before, but never large sheets of ice.

"We should have class down there," Jagree suggested. He was the only one who'd had a chance so far to do more than look at the ice.

"You're suggesting we have school outdoors on a day

like this?" Elic asked.

"We could learn something new."

From their eager grins, Elic could tell the rest of the students were as set on it as Jagree. "All right. Hats and coats back on, and I don't want any complaints about the cold."

He led them to the bank and found a path down to the waterside. The ice extended into the channel about the length of a man's arm from either shore, dark water flowing between. Elic cracked a large chunk loose and held it up. It was almost as clear as glass and shattered like glass when he dropped it. The boys stamped the ice at the water's edge, filling the air with loud crackles and snaps. It didn't look or sound anything like school.

When they had cracked all the ice they could safely reach, he had them gather all the pieces they could carry in their gloved hands. Back at school, they filled a pan with the pieces and Elic set it in front of the fire. He doubted they would be interested in watching ice melt, but they were. It was something new.

Elic warmed up with a bowl of his mother's good chicken soup before heading back for the afternoon class. While they were also interested in ice, the real talk was of the upcoming dance in Bitter Springs, now only a few days off. The older girls giggled and compared dresses. Even the younger children were excited at the notion of visiting another village. Elic was curious about the event himself, though he didn't plan to go. He hadn't danced since childhood and didn't want to look like a fool. More than that, he didn't want to see Sunnea with someone else.

At the end of the day, he walked up to her house. The air was full of snow, kicked up from last night's drifts by a stiff breeze. He shivered. His own warm fireside beckoned, but it was time to make his apologetic speech. He would say only the right things this time, no matter what. Perhaps Sunnea would apologize for her part, too, and they could start over. Or maybe she would greet him so gladly the apology would be unnecessary. Maybe they would fall into each other's arms. Maybe she would be alone in the house ...

Ati answered his knock, scattering his daydream to the wind. "What brings you around, stranger?" From anyone else, he would have taken it as a joke. She wasn't smiling.

"Um ... I had a bath last night and I didn't want to waste it?" It was a stupid thing to say, but it was better than revealing the full extent of the trouble between him and Sunnea.

"So did I, but you don't see me sharing the news," Ati replied.

That picture wasn't quite as compelling as the one he'd formed of Sunnea. "Is Sunnea here? I was hoping to speak with her."

"She and her father went over to Briato's. They should be back soon, if you want to wait."

"Thank you. I will."

"They're trying to find suitable material for a new dress for ... spring."

She gave Elic a hard look. He knew what *spring* meant, but he didn't want to discuss it with anyone except Sunnea. He gave Ati a weak smile. "Briato mentioned he was working on something nice."

She waved him to a chair by the fire. "Tea?" It was a question, though he suspected she would accept only one answer.

"Yes, please." Elic sat without speaking while she poured it. Ati had a prickly personality, but she'd never been this sharp with him, even when he was first courting Sunnea. Had she figured out on her own what was happening, or had Sunnea told her?

Ati brought him the steaming drink and sat across from him with a cup of her own, watching him. "People certainly are all atwitter about this dance in Bitter Springs," she said at last. She spoke the word *dance* as if it tasted foul.

"Yes, all my students are excited about it. Are you and Yshna going?"

She frowned, and Elic was sure he'd said the wrong thing. "Maybe." This answer surprised him. "I'd prefer not to go gallivanting about in this weather, but Yshna wants to keep an eye on his girl. Can't say I blame him." She stared at Elic through narrowed eyes.

Elic tried to smile, though his stomach churned. He was in favor of someone keeping an eye on Sunnea if she was out with anyone besides him.

"I hear you went walking with my niece Kiat," Ati said.

Elic's heart thumped hard, then paused before resuming its normal beat. He'd forgotten all about Kiat's relationship to Sunnea's stepmother. If Sunnea hadn't told her, someone in Kiat's family might have. Or Kiat herself. It was impossible to keep a secret in Deep River ... unless you were Stell. How did she manage it? Elic swallowed the lump in his throat. "It was just a friendly chat. She gave me good advice."

"Is that all she gave you?"

Elic was saved from answering that question when the door opened and Sunnea walked in with her father.

"Of course I like it," she was saying. "But I may not even need a wedding dress."

"The weaving will take time, and so will the sewing," Yshna replied. "I want to do this for you. It doesn't have to be a — oh! Hello, Elic."

Sunnea spun to face him, her cheeks pink. "I ... didn't expect to find you here."

"I can see that." Elic wanted to believe the color in her cheeks came not from the cold but from pleasure at seeing him. Her frown told him otherwise.

Yshna exchanged a glance with Ati over Sunnea's head. Without a word, the couple went into the kitchen and closed the door. Elic stood and crossed the room to where Sunnea stood by the door.

"May I talk to you a moment?"

She hesitated, then said, "No. I'm going to talk to you." She took a deep breath and let it out. "I'm tired — of talk, of waiting, of you, Elic. I thought we could start over, but maybe it's too late."

"If this is about Kiat, I —"

"It's not about Kiat. It's about you. For three months, I looked after you. I listened to your wild talk and tried to understand. I went to see Crane when you wouldn't. And now, when you're finally well again, you can't make up your mind what you want. You say what we had before was only because of the curse. But when I told you I needed time to think about that, you refused to give it to me. You say you want to start over, but you won't even touch me. And yes, it was upsetting to find out you walked out with another woman only one day after our betrothal dinner. How do you think I feel?"

"I know. That's why I want to say —"

Elic's "I'm sorry" wilted on his lips as she plowed

ahead as if he hadn't spoken. "You talk about adventure and how great Crane's life must be. If that's how you feel, why did you even come back?"

"I —"

She opened the door and gestured for him to leave. "Goodbye, Elic."

He stepped out. "But —" The door closed between them.

Didn't she know? Maybe he hadn't told her. When he escaped the curse on that fine summer day, he'd had many thoughts. The first and last were of Sunnea and their future happiness when the curse was broken. He'd been tempted to follow Crane to the end of his quest, and he hadn't wanted to go back under the curse's power. Sunnea was the reason — the only reason — he'd come home. She was the one thing he had been sure of.

Elic turned away from her door and hurried home through the wintry twilight. It wasn't much warmer in his house. He kept his coat on, pulled a chair close to the fire, and tried to think. Sunnea didn't know why he'd come home and hadn't even let him make his apology. She'd told him goodbye. Was it really over?

He stirred the fire into a roaring blaze and sat close to it, escaping into Soorhi's diary while he warmed himself and heated soup for his supper. The next entry was dated almost two years after the previous one.

Look what I found, again! Hardly a moment to think these days, let alone write, but I'm glad to see my old friend again. And I have something worth recording — two things. Young Ordy turns out to be more than a good student and talented acrobat. I always thought there' was some'thing special about him, and the'n the' othe'r day, I looke'd at him and I kne'w: he's got magic in him. With his pare'nts' pe'rmission, I walke'd him up to the' Wizards' Hall today. I hadn't be'e'n the're' since' my one' visit with Dila. It's a long walk, but it was a ple'asant day. Winte'r is almost ove'r. And Ordy is strong. Whe'n his le'gs tire'd, he' trie'd to walk on his hands. He' found the' paving stone's too rough, so he' ran on wall tops and climbe'd tre'e's. Whe'n we' got to the' Wizards' Hall, Ordy was undaunte'd, e've'n at the' ide'a of wizards. I was almost too shy to go inside', but Dillum re'me'mbe're'd me'. He' wasn't surprise'd Dubo had le't me' go, but thought it was for the' be'st. He' se'e'ms to be' in charge'. Maybe' not formally; he' had e've'ryone's re'spe'ct. He' didn't flaunt his powe'r, but once' again, I fe'lt it. He' aske'd Ordy his full name', which turns out to be' Ordahn. He' aske'd a lot of que'stions and taught him a spell — te'sting him, I suppose'. He' thanke'd me' for bringing the' boy and offe're'd to take' him as appre'ntice'. So I was right! He' gave' me' a look like' he' could se'e' right through me' and re'pe'ate'd I was we'lcome' anytime'. That was ve'ry polite', but what would I do among wizards?

Elic nearly flung the book down, frustrated in

retrospect with his teacher. He had visions of the future, he could see what was happening behind his back, he could sense the power in wizards! Yet he seemed unable to recognize his own ability or accept his due from another with magical gifts. Granted, he was still a young man when he wrote this account. Even as an old man, he had never revealed his magical ability.

Elic took a deep breath and let his frustration go. Soorhi had always exuded a quiet confidence that rubbed off on his students. With unfailing generosity, he shared his wisdom and experience. What did it matter if he kept his visions to himself? Elic opened the diary and continued reading.

Dillum introduced us to his former apprentice, a young man named Lok. He's everything I'm not: tall and handsome and, I suspect, good at what he does. I think he knows it, too. He gave us a tour of the Wizards' Hall and showed Ordy some impressive tricks. The boy was quiet on the way home, but I could tell he was excited. His parents were very pleased to hear his report — he has a better future than they ever expected. I left there, and then the second noteworthy event of the day occurred. I heard a familiar voice. I couldn't place it at first. I saw a man walking with an old woman and a boy. The man was my father! I didn't recognize the woman at first, and I didn't know the boy at all, though he looked the right age to be

Ersi, about 14. I crossed the street to get a closer look at them. They didn't know me, of course, with my city clothes, beard, and barbered hair. The boy had Ersi's eyes! Close up, I knew Mom, though she has aged more than Pop. I don't think she is well. I was afraid to speak, for fear of shocking her when she's so frail. I followed them at a distance to find out where they are staying. I will see them again.

Elic's heart raced in sympathy with the barely contained excitement of that entry. Soorhi had given up ever seeing his family again, and then, there they were! The excitement, though, was wrapped up in heartache. Elic tried to imagine meeting his mother in a strange place and not speaking to her, or her not recognizing him. He couldn't picture it. Then again, he also couldn't imagine her aged and frail. He wanted to reach into the diary and comfort the young Soorhi. His gaze fell again on that last line, "I will see them again."

There was a hint of the confidence Elic remembered in his teacher. He wouldn't accept the loss of his family a second time. He clearly planned to do something.

Elic considered his own loss. He preferred action but *doing something* no longer seemed the best way to regain Sunnea's love. Confronting her, explaining, apologizing, all drove her away. Elic's task was more difficult — he had to either give up all hope of reconciliation, or leave it entirely in Sunnea's hands.

Chapter 17. Too Old to Play

Elic slept better than he expected to, waking to an oppressive quiet. It weighed on him like something dire was about to happen. He feared for a moment the curse had returned, but the thought itself revealed it had not. He tried to think something more encouraging, though he couldn't forget the look on Sunnea's face when he'd left her the night before. She'd said she was tired of him. Perhaps it was best to let her go. He'd tried that, only to find she haunted his dreams. Something had changed between them, but they weren't finished with each other yet.

This was no way to start the day. He couldn't *make* her like him again. He couldn't do anything except give her the time she so clearly wanted. He resolved not to think about her at all. He picked up Soorhi's diary in search of a more hopeful story than his own.

> *I took breakfast to my family today. I packed bread and cheese in a basket, with a jug of milk, and took it to their rooming house. I thought if I came to them there, with a gift, and introduced myself calmly, it might be less of a shock. But I was foiled even in this small scheme. The landlord informed me they had left while it was still dark, back to farm country to join the spring work. Now I wish I had spoken up yesterday. Knowing Pop, it wouldn't have kept them here, but at least they'd know I'm alive. Now I'll have to wait until they return next winter. I shared the breakfast with my students, so it didn't go to waste. That's some comfort — these children always appreciate a good meal.*

How like Soorhi to redeem his failure by helping someone else. The entry hadn't made Elic feel any better. He closed the diary. It was time to go to school and light the fire so the building could warm up by the time the students arrived.

Elic stepped out into a morning of shocking cold. The

sky was clear, but the low sun gave no warmth. A keen wind sent yesterday's snow streaming from the crests of drifts. The light powder rippled and slithered along the road. The wind whistled, but the morning seemed too quiet. What sound was missing? The river. How quickly he'd become accustomed to its gentle music. Why would it stop again? As if the dam could rebuild itself overnight.

He hurried to the riverbank and stared at the unfamiliar sight. The flowing water was still there, hidden by a solid, shining sheet of gray ice that reached from bank to bank. Elic hunched in his coat and gazed on this new wonder, but it was too cold to stay outside long. He turned and ran the short distance to the school. His eyes watered with cold, blurring his vision. Was that smoke rising from the chimney?

He entered to find a good fire already blazing. The room was chilly but warming up.

"Morning, Elic."

Elic turned as Jagree came in behind him, his arms laden with firewood. "I should have known." Elic smiled at his brother, his mood warmed as much as the room. "You've just improved my whole day."

"I was up early to check on the horses at Auntie Stell's." Jagree dumped his load in the woodbox and backed up to the fire. "I hope I'm not the only one to show up!"

The morning class was smaller than usual. The other two boys who lived in the village bundled up and made the brave dash to school. Elic worried about Lafa who had so much farther to travel, but it soon became clear he had stayed home. The remaining boys abandoned their assigned seats and gathered as close as possible to the fire to swap stories about their perilous trek to school.

"Did you see the river?" Rynk asked. "I threw a rock at it, and it just skittered across the surface."

"Pap says this cold will freeze a horse's breath in its nostrils," Jagree commented. "And Mam says the wind will chap the skin right off your face."

Elic wasn't sure whether they were exaggerating. Extreme cold could be dangerous if you weren't prepared, and he was relieved Lafa had elected not to risk it. A severe cold snap was not unusual, though this one had come early in the season.

The afternoon class was also reduced. Ylani, like her brother Lafa, was absent, as were Foli, Alill, and Young Myn, who lived at the far end of the village. Kiat escorted Brynnit. When she made as if to leave, Elic invited her to stay awhile. "At least warm up before you go out again."

She held her hands out to the fire. "I'll spend the afternoon, if you don't mind. Stell doesn't need me till later, and it seems warmer here than at home."

"Ma scolded us for tracking in snow," Brynnit explained in a loud whisper.

This class also gathered close to the fire and talked about the weather and other news. After the initial burst of chatter, the older girls grew subdued.

"What if it doesn't warm up before the dance?" Silib asked.

She was only ten, and Elic didn't understand her interest in the event. There had been so much excitement about it, though, it was natural some of it had rubbed off on the younger children. He had no answer to her question. He supposed the people of Bitter

Springs might cancel or postpone their winter dance in the case of extremely severe weather. It seemed unlikely they would postpone it for the benefit of Deep River.

He nurtured a fleeting hope the dance would be cancelled. If that happened, Sunnea couldn't go with Huvro or Rovhi. Kiat raised an eyebrow at him and smiled slightly as if she could read his mind. He shook his head, scattering the selfish idea. Hadn't he resolved not to think of Sunnea? Even if the dance were cancelled, it wouldn't solve anything.

"I doubt this cold will last," he said. It was just a guess to direct the children back to their lessons. Some wizards could control the weather, but even Soorhi with his visions couldn't accurately predict it.

When Elic left school that afternoon, shouts and laughter floated from the direction of the river. He returned to the bank and watched bundled-up children sliding on the ice. He recognized Jagree's coat and guessed the three smaller figures were Senri, Foli, and Myn, though he couldn't tell one from another through all the layers. Rynk was probably out there, too. Two figures in dresses were probably Kiat and Brynnit, judging by height. The little girl clung to her sister as she pulled her over the ice. The boys ran and slid, fell, scrambled up and fell again, laughing uproariously. They didn't appear to feel the bumps or mind the cold.

"Elic!" Jagree called. "Join us!"

He edged down the steep path to the riverside. He needed some simple fun in his life, and sliding on the ice would be a new experience. He stepped onto the smooth surface. His feet slid from under him, and he fell with a jarring crash. The ice creaked and groaned ominously, which bothered him more than possible bruises. He scrambled back to shore on all fours.

"Are you going to play or not?" Jagree asked.

"I'm too heavy."

"Come on, you're not that much bigger than I am."

"Yes, I am. Besides, I'm not dressed for it."

Elic returned home, sorry for himself. He was too old to play, and it was too cold to stand outside and watch. It was cold in the house, too, and he was starting to feel hungry. And there wasn't even anyone waiting for him with a hot meal or a warm embrace.

He built up his banked fire and considered. A fresh, hot meal in a warm room was tempting — either at Mam's or at the Heron — but he didn't want to venture out again. The brief dash on the ice had chilled him through. He was thankful now for the big pot of soup Mam had brought him. He'd left it covered on the porch, according to her instructions. He'd had one supper and two lunches from it already, dipping the cold soup into a smaller pot to heat. Now the remainder was frozen solid. He brought the whole pot in to thaw and heat up.

While the soup heated, he returned to Soorhi's diary, hoping to read of some good coming from the man's loss.

I am so proud of my students. Each one is at a different level, but the more advanced help the beginners, and they are all making excellent progress. I only wish I could give them more — books, paper, paint, musical instruments! As it is, I'm forever sharing my food with them, or buying shoes for a child whose family has fallen on hard times. Harder than usual, I mean. I'm out nearly e'very night, appe'aling to pote'ntial subscribe'rs. The'se' e've'nts look like' partie's. To me', they are' hard work. I fe'el out of place' with fine' pe'ople'. I'm much more' comfortable' with my stude'nts' familie's. They're' not swamp pe'ople', but they're' not far from it. Many are' displace'd country pe'ople', victims of too many faile'd crops, too much bad we'athe'r. Ye't e've'n with the'm, plain frie'ndly conve'rsation se'e'ms too much to ask. They don't say as much, but I can se'e' it: they se't me' above' the'm. They don't re'alize' how haphazard my e'ducation has be'e'n. Some'time's I'm te'mple'd to visit the' Wizards' Hall for a chat with Dillum, or e've'n Lok. How would that look? Dillum's invitation tickle'd me', but he' was just be'ing polite'. As if my little' visions made' me' a wizard!

There he went again, dismissing his gift. Why did it matter what gift he had, or didn't? It looked like the thing Soorhi needed most was a friend. Why not Dillum, or another wizard? Elic lacked even a hint of magical talent, yet he had been friends with a wizard for years — a powerful one, as it turned out. Their friendship began before anyone suspected Crane's abilities. Elic had been the strong one. By the time Crane's power became apparent, their friendship was a settled thing. It was impossible to imagine how they might have gotten along if they hadn't met until then.

All Elic knew was he missed Crane. Would Crane still

be his friend, if — no, *when* — they met again? Elic
hoped so. Maybe someday Crane would come home and
share stories of his heroic adventures. That would be
good. Maybe he would have enough adventures for two.

The bubbling soup rattled its lid. Elic took it off the
fire and dished up a bowl. He continued reading while
he ate. After a gap of several months, the diary took up
again with an entry dated in late fall of that same year.

*Whene'er I go out, I watch for my family, and
today I finally saw them! At least, I saw Pop and
Ersi. I wonde'red about Mom, though I have' a
pretty good ide'a what happene'd. She' wasn't well
last winte'r. I followe'd the'm to a rooming house'
not far from me'. At least one' of my stude'nts live's
the're'. This time', I we'nt right up to the'ir room
and knocke'd on the' door. Pop answe're'd, looking
ve'ry suspicious. Ye's, a familiar e'xpre'ssion. He'
hasn't change'd, e'xce'pt he' is stoope'd and shrunke'n.
I re'me'mbe'r him as a towe'ring figure', ye't he' had
to look up at me', and I'm not a tall man. He'
wouldn't le't me' in, e've'n afte'r I told him my name'.
He' said, "I have' only one' son," and close'd the'
door. Through the' door, I he'ard Ersi ask, "Who
was that?" and Pop's reply: "No one' you know."
I gue'ss it's up to me' to make' sure' he' doe's know.*

Elic paged ahead in the little book. After this followed
a flurry of brief entries written close together. Day-to-

day life had often prevented Soorhi from writing in his diary, but for events involving his family, he always found time to record them. Elic ladled more soup into his bowl and continued with the next long entry.

I had a vision about Ersi this morning, the' first in ye'ars. I re'membere'd to use' the' liste'ning te'chnique' the' Aklaka practice', and I think it helpe'd make' the' vision cle'are'r and longe'r. I saw Ersi at the' marke't ne'ar he're', at the' booth with the' blue'-stripe'd awning. He' was alone', and I was sure' I could me'e't him the're' without Pop knowing. I got up right away and we'nt the're', and only the'n did I re'alize' I didn't know whe'n he' might come'. I couldn't wait all day, but I did have' some' time' be'fore' school. And why would the' vision show me' an appointme'nt I couldn't ke'e'p? I had to trust it. The'n he' came'. He' was asking the' price' of drie'd plums, Pop's favorite' as I re'call. He' turne'd away without buying. That's whe'n I took my chance'. "You're' not ge'tting anything?" I aske'd. "At the'se' price's?" he' re'torte'd. He's a good-looking fellow, and almost my he'ight alre'ady. He' looks more' like' Mom than Pop. "Le't me'," I said, and bought a sack of plums for him, and one' for my class. We' walke'd away toge'the'r. "Why he'lp me', rich man?" he' wante'd to know. "I'm not a rich man," I said. "Only your brothe'r." He' stoppe'd walking and stared at me. "Soorhi?" he whispered. So I was surprised, too. How did he know my name? It seems Mom had tried to keep my memory alive, telling Ersi stories about his lost brother, even when Pop told her not to. As I suspected, she died last spring, before they even got over the mountains. Ersi wanted her to stay here and get well. She wouldn't leave Pop. Sometimes there's no explaining other people's choices. I showed Ersi where my school is. He wouldn't come in, but he said he might visit. Maybe I can get him to enroll, if I'm patient.

Elic closed the diary and rested his head on it a moment. At last, some good news in Soorhi's tale. His mother had died, and his father regarded him as dead, but at least he had his brother again. Elic had to remind himself these events had taken place long ago, before his own parents were born; perhaps even before his grandparents. Yet the grief and the joy were real. Elic's own problems shrank in comparison. Here he was, eating his mother's good soup. He was on good terms with his father. He saw his brother every day and had the privilege of watching him grow up. He might have lost his sweetheart, but his town was returning to life. How could he complain?

Chapter 18. Too Cold for School

The bitter cold continued into the next day, and this time, Elic didn't see any welcoming smoke rise from the school's chimney. He hurried inside and shut the door, though it made little difference. With no fire burning, indoors was nearly as cold as out. Elic pulled off his gloves to build a fire, but the woodbox was almost empty. He braced himself for a trip to the woodpile. When he stepped out again, his face ached with cold. He pitied anyone who couldn't avoid going out in this weather and hoped the farm children would have the sense to stay at home again.

He found the stack of firewood depleted — not enough

fuel to keep the school warm through a second extremely cold day. It only made sense to give all his students a day off, not only the farm children. And the next day would be a holiday because of the dance. With luck, the weather would improve, at least enough that the fuel supply would last until the woodcutter could bring more.

He tacked a note to the door:

School closed today. Warm up at my house' if you need to. —Elic.

That would alert anyone who might come to the school before he could get the message out, though he hoped it wouldn't be necessary. He went home long enough to throw on an extra shirt and wrap a scarf around his neck. Sunnea had made it for him when she was learning to knit a few years back. Before they were courting, though no one had questioned whether they someday would be. The scarf was an obvious beginner's project, lumpy and oddly shaped, but soft and warm. Warmer than their interactions in recent days. Elic recalled again the simple warmth when Sunnea sat beside him on his front step after Crane flew away. He wished he could return to that day. He would hold her hand and thank her for her kindness while he was ill. It was probably too late to do that now. If he tried, would she even listen to him?

Bundled up, he ventured out into the village. The low sun cast his shadow ahead of him down the empty road. He stopped at each home with children, beginning at Toli the cobbler's. It was only a few steps from his own house, but his face was already numb from the wind.

"Don't come to school this afternoon, Liko," Elic said

when the boy answered his knock. "It's closed today."

"Hooray!"

"Don't listen to him," Kolma said. "He'll be bored before the day's out."

"No, I won't! We're going to play on the ice again."

"Are you sure you want to go out?" Elic asked. "This wind will freeze your face."

"No, it won't! Mama, where's my scarf?"

"Hanging over the end of your bed," she said. "Children hardly feel the cold when they're playing. I doubt they'll stay out long, though. Will you come in and warm yourself?"

"Thank you, but I need to keep going," Elic replied.

He pulled his scarf over his mouth and nose before he continued to the next house and the next with his message, up one side of the road to the end of the village, then back down the other.

At Sinth the carpenter's house, Senri cheered, but Silib frowned. "Why can't we have school? I promised Myn and Foli I'd help them learn to spell."

"There might not be enough wood to heat the school in this cold," Elic explained. "And I won't have more until next week."

"We don't mind if it's cold! We could wear our hats!"

"It's probably only for one day," he assured her. "You'll have plenty of chances to teach Myn and Foli how to spell."

At Briato's house, Kiat answered the door. "Come to take me walking again?" she asked with a mischievous grin.

"I thought you said I couldn't." At least they could joke about it.

She chuckled. "That's right, I did. And we don't want to make Sunnea jealous."

"I'm not sure it matters anymore. That's not what I came about, though. Will you let Brynnit know school's cancelled today?"

"But yesterday was such fun!" Kiat said.

Her mother came to the door. "No school? Then you girls can help me today."

"I'm already helping Pa!" Brynnit called from behind a large loom. She peeked around the frame and smiled at Elic.

He walked over to see what she was working on. The loom dwarfed her, and the shuttle seemed outsized in her small hand. She worked with patience and a smile, weaving a blanket with brown and yellow stripes.

"That's very good," Elic said. "Did you do all this yourself?"

"Pa started it, but I've done more. I think it looks like a bee."

"You're right, it does." Next to Brynnit, Briato's loom was producing something finer, a creamy linen with blue stripes. Elic didn't comment on it. "I'll be on my way now. School should be open again after a day or two." He stepped back out into the cold.

Soon, only his parents' house remained. He stopped in the forge but didn't see his brother.

"Morning, Pap," he called over the fire's roar. It was warmer there than any place he'd been all morning. "Is Jagree around?"

"Try the stable — he's probably visiting his friends," Pap said. "Unless I can help you?"

"I'm cancelling school today. We burned most of the wood yesterday."

Pap nodded. "Too cold to think! Or much of anything else. There won't be a market today, either."

"That could be a problem," Elic said. "I'm running low on food."

"I expect your mother will take care of you," Pap said with a fond smile. "Thinking of your schoolhouse, a little stove would be more efficient than that open fire. I'll make you one after I finish Sunnea's cookstove."

"Maybe you could make it first," Elic suggested.

"The cookstove is nearly finished. I think it will make your bride happy."

What if the only thing that made her happy was to not be his bride? Elic forced a smile and left the forge. The cold hit him even more intensely by comparison, and he was glad he had only to cross the road. On his way into the stable, he passed a covered cart he'd never seen before. That meant Stell had guests, even in this weather.

It wasn't as warm in the stable as at the forge, but warmer than outdoors, and sheltered from the wind. The dim space smelled of hay and manure, with the sharp tang of horse sweat.

"Jagree? No school today," he called. "But some of the boys were going to play on the ice again, if you're interested."

"Thanks," Jagree's voice replied from one of the stalls. Elic peered in that direction and made out the shapes of two horses in the dim light.

As Elic left the stable, his stomach rumbled. It was hard work just staying upright in the wind and cold, and his stomach complained that it had been a long time since breakfast. Instead of going home, he stopped at the inn to warm up. Stell was serving breakfast to three strangers.

"Good morning, Auntie Stell. That smells good. Spare some for a freezing teacher?"

"I made plenty. Have a seat."

He sat at the long table with the other guests.

"These fellows are musicians," Stell said. "They were passing through on their way back to Sweetwater, but they decided to spend another day rather than travel in this cold." She served him sweetened porridge and a slice of fried ham.

"We're *from* Sweetwater. We're on our way to Bitter Springs," one of the men corrected her. He was tall and thin with a wild mop of yellow hair. He didn't appear any older than Elic. "We're supposed to play for their winter dance tomorrow, so we'll have to leave in the morning no matter what the weather does. After that, we can go home and den up for the rest of the winter."

"Too bad a certain someone isn't here to change the weather for us," Elic joked. Stell's eyes widened, and her cheeks flushed. "Didn't I hear Crane had learned to work weather?" he added, unnerved by her reaction.

"Crane! Yes, he did." She relaxed some, though her laughter seemed forced. "That's exactly the sort of help we need."

The oldest of the guests gazed appreciatively at Stell. "Will you be at the dance?"

"I couldn't close the inn. I might miss an overnight guest."

"Are you expecting someone?" Elic asked.

"Of course not! How could I?" She blushed again, as if she knew more than she was telling.

"As long as you'll be open, I'll probably come for supper," he said.

"You're not going to the dance? I thought all the young fellows would be there."

"All but one."

*

Elic hated to leave the cozy inn, but he returned home after his breakfast. He stirred his fire into a blaze. The morning rang with shouts and laughter of children sliding on the ice while Elic huddled close to the hearth, reading Soorhi's diary.

Ersi came'! I wasn't sure' whether to expect him. It was a sunny day and mild for the' season, so I sent the' children outside' at lunchtime', and he' came' up to the' gate'. He' hesitated until I invited him to come' eat with me'. He' had his lunch and sat with me' on the' step but wouldn't come' inside'. He' told me' about his job. He' delivers messages, both business notes and love' letters. He's fast and he' can't read, so people' trust him. I tried to explain why I want to teach these' children. He' looked puzzled. "What good does it do them?" I pointed out the' boy who wants to be' governor, the' girl who wants to have' her own shop, the' three' boys who want to sail on a ship to lands they never heard of before' they came' here'. I'm not sure' he' understood — he' thinks it pointless to raise' their hopes, but a little' hope' can go a long way.

Elic stopped reading to ponder that thought. Like Ersi, he had questioned the value of what he was teaching the children of Deep River. What good did it do them, really, knowing how to read, write, and figure? They had limited reading matter, and until recently, little reason to write letters. Counting and calculating might come in handy for some, but how much did they *need* it? Perhaps he would never know. He wondered if Soorhi's students had done the great things they'd dreamed of. Although he couldn't speak for those in Eukard City, at least one in Deep River had — Crane. Soorhi didn't live to see that, but he'd expected it. He'd had faith he was doing good.

Elic continued reading, an entry written several days later.

> *Ersi come's e'very day now. He' won't come' inside' — the' school se'tting make's him ne'rvous. That must be' Pop's influe'nce'. I hinte'd he' could e'nroll, or e'ven just visit a class, but he' wouldn't he'ar of it. Maybe' it would be' difficult, starting at his age'. I won't me'ntion it again. I don't want to scare' him off.*

The next entry began on the same page, dated weeks later, in the early spring. There was no explanation of the gap this time, but Elic imagined Soorhi was busy running the school, getting to know his brother, and raising support in the evenings. It was lucky he wrote in the diary at all.

> *Ersi is gone' again. I trie'd to pe'rsuade' him to stay with me', but he' wouldn't. He's more' like' Pop than he'll admit. At le'ast he' se'eme'd happy to know me'. I am glad to know him at last, and I hope' he'll come' back ne'xt winte'r. He' hardly says a word, ye't he' is good company. I'm going to miss that.*

Elic recalled the hours he had spent in Crane's company, mostly silent, but communicating, nonetheless. And even Sunnea, though she talked more than Crane, had often been content to stroll at his side in quiet understanding. He missed that. Lately, they'd been doing more talking and less understanding.

Elic didn't want to do anything that took him away from the warm fireside. He fed the fire, heated the last of the soup for lunch, and continued reading. Months passed before the next entry, a long one dated in late summer.

I fear I've made a big mistake, though it seemed like a good idea at the time. After Ersi left, I worked up my courage and went to the Wizards' Hall, just for a little conversation. Although I was nervous, Dillum answered my knock and made me feel at home. I thought the place would be full of mysterious figures doing mysterious deeds, but they're a varied lot. A few do have great powers — to light fire with a look or change the weather or their own form — but there are also a lot of modest types: healers, finders, and such. Dillum is the greatest of them, though he never lords it over anyone. He always has time for me, and thinks highly of young Ordy — Ordahn, I should say. But back to my mistake — after a few weeks of visiting, I felt comfortable among the magic folk, though my little gift is the most modest of all. I was making friends. Lok sometimes let me into his circle of young wizards. They're far cleverer and more learned than I, and Lok is the cleverest and most powerful of the lot. Sometimes they challenge each other, flinging and deflecting spells of greater and greater intensity until something gets broken and the older wizards ask them to stop. It starts in fun. I'm not sure it always ends that way. I mostly kept my mouth shut and stayed out of the way. I was chattier with the women. Especially a young healer, Kubi, a country girl new to the city. She doesn't call herself a wizard; none of the women do, though I suspect she and some others have at least as much power as Lok and his friends. Kubi is full of good sense and talent. She reminds me a little of Clover. Lok tried and failed — repeatedly — to seduce her. At the time, I thought this very funny — usually he gets any girl he wants, but the naive little country girl wouldn't be blinded by good looks and power. I think now laughing at him was the start of the trouble. Last night, Dillum and I were sitting on a bench in the herb garden, enjoying the summer evening and talking about my visions. He actually seemed interested in them! Lok came along, sullen and snorting. He insulted Kubi's intelligence, and Dillum teased him a little about how she wouldn't warm his bed. Lok maintained that wasn't it; she was stupid because she proposed treating hives with nettles. "Imagine rubbing a sting on a welt!" he said.

I had heard of such a remedy, years ago when I was wandering and talking to hermits. Fool that I am, I spoke up. "You don't rub it," I said. They both looked at me like I was a talking cat. "You don't rub it on, you cook and eat it. I've seen it work." If I'd had the sense to stop there, it probably would have been fine. Lok doesn't appreciate being told he's wrong — he stomped off in a huff — though given a chance to cool off, he might have been grateful for the information. But I couldn't let him insult Kubi. And maybe I'm full of myself, too. I had to add, "Your ignorance doesn't make Kubi stupid." Something told me to duck. I threw myself off the bench and a hot wind stood my hair on end. With my eyes closed, I saw sparkles like sunlight on snow. Dillum scolded Lok, who didn't have anything to say, for once. Apparently, he'd attacked me with some sort of spell. He usually reserves his temper for his equals, so I suppose I should be flattered. At the time, I was shaken. Why would he attack me? Did I insult him that badly? Dillum guessed he was jealous about Kubi. Jealous of me? That's hard to picture. I didn't notice any injuries, though. Dillum couldn't tell me what the spell was, but knowing Lok as he does, he guessed it could have stopped my ears or my mouth … or my heart. Good thing I ducked! Lok was gone by then, and I was just as glad. The spell's only lasting *effect seemed to be exhaustion. I staggered home and went to bed. When I woke this morning, my vision was blurred. It's not that bad, but it happened overnight. I don't think this is the result of too much reading by poor light. I think I'm going blind. I think I've been cursed.*

Elic had to read the last line again. Soorhi, cursed? He'd never mentioned it. He had revealed much about Deep River and the school and Yrae's Curse. Not this secret about himself.

Elic glanced at the date on the entry and did a rough calculation. Soorhi was only twenty-five or so when this happened to him, and around sixty when he came to Deep River. A lot could have happened in that time. Maybe he was wrong about the curse, or maybe it was lifted. Certainly, it hadn't had the effect Soorhi predicted. The Soorhi Elic knew was not a blind man.

Was he?

Elic turned to the next entry, dated a few days later, eager to learn how events unfolded.

I let my fear keep me away from the Wizards' Hall for two days. When my vision did not improve, I went back to see what could be done. Kubi confirmed I had a magical injury but couldn't do anything about it. Lok used a complicated spell of his own devising; Kubi feared picking it apart could make my condition worse. Dillum agreed. Only Lok can lift this curse.

Unfortunately, he has not been back to the Wizards' Hall since that night. It is against the rules of magic to use it against someone who is no threat and has not consented to duel. Punishment consists of having one's own magic removed, temporarily for a first offense, then permanently. I didn't know that was possible. It sounds unpleasant. Lok is choosing to avoid punishment by running rather than by restoring me. This curse, though, could be a lot worse. Maybe it will take years to lose my sight completely, and at least I'm alive. For now, I can still see well enough to read and write. The children shouldn't be able to tell. I don't want them to know — it would be too hard to explain, and I'm not sure their parents would trust me. I'll have to adjust. This is my new life.

Elic smiled. That was Soorhi's refrain throughout the diary. Every time he settled down to something different, he pronounced it his new life, as if it were a permanent arrangement. Yet he was never too disturbed over drastic change. He simply accepted it. Elic wondered if he would ever be able to adjust so readily. The end of Yrae's Curse was the biggest change he'd ever experienced. So far, he wasn't proud of his response. His thoughtless words and deeds had driven Sunnea away. He was glad to see the curse broken. He was not yet ready to accept his new life.

Chapter 19. Secrets of the Dead and the Living

By afternoon, the bitter chill had chased even the hardiest ice sliders indoors. The silence and the cold seemed to press against Elic's back. He sat with his feet almost in the flames. Most of the heat disappeared up the chimney, drawing cold air over his spine. Now he wished Pap's cookstove were not only finished but installed. On a day like this, he would have married Sunnea for that alone. If she would have him.

For most of the brief day, sunshine streamed through

the windows. It brought enough light to read by, though no warmth. As daylight dimmed and he had to squint to see what Soorhi had written, Elic left his fireside only long enough to light the lamp so he could continue. The next entry was dated several weeks after Soorhi's fateful encounter with Lok. The handwriting was noticeably larger now, but still neat.

I don't know what to think. Some time ago, I advertised for a second teacher, so I could separate the boys and girls. The older ones distract each other, and not much learning takes place.

Elic chuckled and nodded in agreement. The arrangement in Deep River had its origin all those years ago in Soorhi's first school. With only one teacher for the whole school, first Soorhi and now Elic divided the day as well as the children, though it was the same idea. But maybe the idea needed adjustment now.

Only a few candidates responded, none of them right for the job. The ones who were willing to do it for what I could pay did not live up to my standards. I was ready to give up when a young woman appeared at my door. At first, I thought she must have come to the wrong place. I may not see perfectly, but I could tell she was well dressed, and I guessed she was pretty. She seemed familiar, though I didn't recognize her until she introduced herself: Dila! She' flatte'red me' by be'ing happy to see' me'. At only e'ighte'en, she's a little' younge'r than I had in mind, but e'xactly what I was hoping for in e've'ry othe'r way. She' ke'pt studying on he'r own afte'r he'r fathe'r se'nt me' away; she' e've'n taught he'r frie'nds! She' says this is just the' sort of work she' wants to do. As if that we're'n't e'nough, she' knows the' sort of pe'ople' who could subscribe', and she' has he'r own mode'st fortune'. If I pay he'r, she' vows to re'turn the' full amount to ope'rating the' school. Alre'ady she' has plans to buy the' building and e'xpand it. She' has so much e'ne'rgy, she' make's me' dizzy!

Elic smiled about that. He suspected it wasn't only her energy that caused Soorhi's dizziness. He was still getting used to the idea Soorhi had noticed women, but it wasn't the shock it had been in the beginning. There was his boyish devotion to Clover, his fleeting infatuation with the young Aklaka woman, his friendship with the healer, Kubi. And hadn't he wished to meet someone like Dila, only older? Here she was herself, grown up and happy to see him — what could be better?

Both in the diary and in Deep River, Soorhi had seemed content with his solitary life. Yet Elic hoped that wasn't all he had ever known. Several short entries followed, not about anything obviously important, full of "Dila this" and "Dila that." Elic turned to the next long entry with mingled joy and trepidation, living the story alongside Soorhi. Would there be love in Soorhi's life?

Had there been?

> *Ersi is back, alone'. Pop finally worke'd himself to de'ath. I wasn't all that surprise'd and can't work up much grie'f ove'r the' man who cast me' out. I do grie've' that Ersi is on his own so e'arly in life'. Now I'm all the' family he' has le'ft. Dila worke'd out how to carve' some' private' space' for him from my quarte'rs, so he' won't have' to spe'nd his funds on a room. I'm glad to have' him, and she' se'ems fond of him, too. They're' close' in age' but she' acts like' his mothe'r. What did I e've'r do without he'r?*

Elic turned the page, expecting more details on what he did *with* her. It seemed clear they were well suited and a good team. He wanted to read a love story with a happy ending, even if it had happened long ago. His expectation of a continuing story was disappointed. Soorhi had never been a consistent diarist, and the next entry was dated three months later, towards the end of winter.

> *I hope'd Ersi would stay in Eukard City now, but I looke'd in his room this morning, and he' and his things we're' gone'. Of course', the're' was no note' — he' still can't write'. He' doe'sn't know any life' except this, and it looks like' he' doe'sn't want any othe'r. We'll, he'll be' back ne'xt winte'r. Ersi, Dila and I we're' like' a family, and I hope' we' will be'*

again. I just looked at what I wrote' there' — Dila and I we're' like' a family. How I wish it we're' true'! Dare' I write' that I love' he'r? The' se'ven years be'twe'en our age's are' not the' obstacle' they we're' before' she' came' of age'. But I have' nothing to offe'r an accomplishe'd young woman — no we'alth, no position, no powe'r. I'm half blind alre'ady, and sure' to ge't worse'. I can't le't he'r know how I fe'el. I must ke'ep it to myself. I shouldn't e'ven write' about it. That's my ne'w life'.

Elic flipped through the next several pages. True to his word, Soorhi didn't write about his feelings for Dila, or much else. Several years fit into those few pages, the handwriting larger and more scrawled over time. The entries were brief, mostly concerning Ersi's arrivals and departures. Dila was mentioned only indirectly, as the girls' teacher.

Elic didn't know what to think. Where was the adventurous young man who sought out hermits and lived among Mountain Folk? Where was the determined teacher who started his own school when he couldn't find an existing one to suit him? According to his own diary, Soorhi had never shied from trying new things or doing what he must, even if it was uncomfortable. But when he loved a woman who was a perfect fit for him, he wouldn't risk telling her. He said it was because he had nothing to offer. Elic wondered if there was more to it. What did he fear — that she wouldn't love him? Or that she would?

This couldn't be the end of it, but according to the dates in the diary, Soorhi stopped writing for about twenty years between these brief fragments and the next long entry. There had been long gaps before. Maybe he had lost the book again. Or maybe, if he had to leave love out of it, there was no story worth telling.

Elic closed the book. His eyes hurt, and he was hungry. He checked the soup pot; he'd emptied it at lunch. It seemed a long time since that last bowl of soup, and even longer since breakfast at the inn. The inn — his mouth watered at the thought of one of Stell's suppers. He would brave the cold for it. He layered on his warm clothes again and walked up to the Heron.

The air was frigid, but the wind had died down. It puffed fitfully rather than whistling around corners. Clouds covered the stars, and Elic wondered if it might snow again. A heavy snowfall might keep people away from the dance as effectively as extreme cold. Then Sunnea —

You're not thinking about the dance, and you're not thinking about her, he reminded himself. *You're going to supper, and that's all.*

The inn was comparatively empty for the time of day. The three musicians were still there, playing a dice game with a few hardy locals. It appeared most of the regulars were sticking close to their own firesides. Elic sat by himself, though there was plenty of room at the big communal tables. Even if he wasn't thinking about Sunnea, he had plenty to occupy his mind. The way Soorhi recorded events made it seem they had occurred one on top of the other, with no respite between. He'd found, lost, and refound his family, opened a school, suffered Lok's curse, fallen in love — enough activity for several lives — but none of these things had been part of his life in Deep River. And there were those cryptic references late in the diary that had so baffled Elic when he first picked it up. He thought he knew the old man, but he had hidden most of his early experiences. Had he shared his story with anyone? It would have to be someone who could keep a secret.

"I thought you said you'd come by tomorrow night," Stell said. She gave him a steaming mug of mulled ale.

"You'll see me then, too." Elic sipped appreciatively from the warm drink.

"If you join the others, you might win supper off that fiddler. He's bound to lose eventually!"

Elic shook his head. "I'm no gambler. I think I'll stay here. May I ask you something, though? If anyone knows, you would."

"What is it?"

"Did Soorhi ever have a family here? A wife, children?"

She stared at him for a long moment. "A wife? Not that I know of," she said at last. "Why?"

"I've been reading his diary. It's full of things he never told me. In a late entry, he wrote that Crane reminded him of his 'little fellow.' I thought he might have had a son."

Stell gave him a piercing look. "No, his little fellow wasn't his son," she replied with certainty. Her expression softened. "When did he write that about Crane?"

"After the accident," Elic said. "It seems he expected something to happen. He had ... visions."

She nodded thoughtfully. "He was always interested in Crane."

Elic hid his disappointment that Soorhi had failed to make a life with Dila or anyone else. It was foolish to feel someone else's loss so deeply, especially a loss that had happened more than sixty years ago to a man who was now dead. But he couldn't help it.

"Is there anything else you want?" Stell asked.

"Yes. A woman's opinion." Elic drew a steadying breath and forced himself to speak. "If a man loves someone but he doesn't believe he's good enough for her, should he tell her, anyway?"

She drew back, a startled look in her eyes. Why did everything he said to her provoke this reaction? She'd been acting oddly ever since Crane left. Now she smiled, with a dreamy, faraway look. "Yes," she sighed. "He should tell her. There's no way he can guess how she feels, and she might surprise him." She turned her gaze back to Elic. "May I bring your supper now?" Her voice was brisk, all dreaminess gone.

"Yes, please. I'm famished!"

"It's the cold weather." She went into the kitchen and came back with a steaming plate of chicken stew. The aroma made his mouth water.

He forked up a chunk of potato and nearly burned his mouth. It was so delicious and warming, he hardly cared. He took his time over the meal, in no hurry to go back out into the cold. Stell had provided more than food, drink, and her opinion. She had given him even more to wonder about. Forget about Soorhi's secrets; what was *she* hiding?

Chapter 20. The Little Fellow

Although freezing weather continued into the next day, the cold wasn't as brutal. After a late breakfast, Elic walked to his parents' house to return Mam's soup pot. Most of the snow had blown away, though a few drifts remained against the walls of houses. Shouts and laughter rose from the river, where children enjoyed one more free day on the ice.

"It looks like the girls will get their dance, after all," Mam said. She took the pot from him and gathered fresh bread and other food to send home with him. He didn't even have to ask. "I'm glad. I was looking forward to it myself."

"Are you going?" Elic tried to sound casual.

"Yes, do you want to ride with us? You and —"

"I probably won't go," he said. "I'll have supper at the Heron. Someone should keep Stell company."

"You and Jagree, then," Mam said. "I tried to talk her into closing for one night, but she wouldn't hear of it. I suppose it makes sense now that she has overnight guests again. It's a shame she'll miss all the fun."

Pap grinned. "Maybe she's meeting someone in secret."

"Oh, you!" Mam gave him a playful shove.

He grabbed her hand and kissed it. "May I have this dance, pretty miss?"

They'd always seemed a well-matched pair, but Elic had never seen them act so young. He left them laughing and playing in their kitchen.

As he closed the door behind him, an ear-splitting yell rang out from the direction of the river. Not the shout of children at play, but of a child in trouble. Elic dropped the food bundle and raced across the road, past the inn, and down a rough path worn into the bank. Only Senri, Foli, and Young Myn remained on the ice, with no adults or older children watching. As Elic reached the riverside, Senri and Foli scurried to shore, scattering droplets from the thin layer of water on the surface. They shouted for Myn to join them.

"What's wrong?" Elic asked.

"The ice cracked," Foli said. "Myn's too scared to move."

The ice groaned and Myn wailed. Elic knew little

more about ice than these six-year-olds. But he was the only adult around. He had to do something — what, though? For now, the ice under Myn was solid, but a web of cracks broke the smooth surface.

"Myn? Can you come to me?" Elic held out his arms. The boy shook his head. His foot shifted and a zig-zag line crackled across the ice. "Stay calm," Elic said, struggling to control the frantic tremor in his voice. "I'll come to you."

As Elic set one foot on the ice, a hand caught his arm and held him back. "You're too heavy," Jagree said. "I'll go."

"I'm not that much bigger than you, remember?" Elic jerked his arm away, but Jagree hung on. He really wasn't much smaller than Elic now, and strong for his age. Elic couldn't break out of his grip.

While they struggled, the ice broke. A slab tilted under Myn. The boy screamed as he slid sideways into the water. Behind them, Foli shrieked in wordless panic.

"Myn! I'm coming!" Elic shouted.

"No, I am!" Jagree yelled.

Elic tried again to shake out of Jagree's grasp. Before he could break loose, an eagle stooped out of the sky and sank its talons into the back of Myn's coat, dragging him away from the hole. The big bird strained to lift the child. Myn was a small boy, but several times heavier than a river fish. He slipped and fell, dragging the eagle down with him. The boy struggled to regain his footing, which cracked the ice even more. The eagle refused to let go, though they both might end up in the water.

Elic freed himself and dashed onto the ice while Jagree's attention was on the child and the eagle. He immediately broke through into frigid water almost to his waist. He plunged ahead, fighting the current and the cold. It wasn't far, but he feared he would never reach Myn before the boy was swept away. The eagle strained its wings until Elic grasped the boy. It released its talons and flew into the air. Elic held Myn above the water and fought his way back to shore.

Myn howled. He was wet and freezing, though otherwise unharmed. "I'll take him to the inn," Elic said to Jagree. "You fetch Mam. Foli, Senri — go home!"

Jagree ran up the path. Elic staggered behind him, carrying the weeping boy. His own legs and feet were soaked and numb. He kept his eyes on the path and tried to climb quickly. At the top of the bank, he bumped into someone.

"Oh! Excuse me!" she said.

Sunnea?

"Sorry," Elic puffed.

"It's all right," she said. "What's going on? Can I help?"

"Get Old Myn," Elic said through chattering teeth. She stepped aside so he could pass. He lugged his burden toward the inn.

"I told you I saw an eagle," she called after him. "I'm sure it's the same one." She pointed toward the roof of the inn.

The eagle perched there, glaring down at him. He recalled the day the curse was lifted, and Crane flew away from Deep River. She was right about what she'd seen, and he was wrong. Maybe not only this time. He stared back at the eagle. "Thanks," he said, and went inside.

Myn had stopped crying by this time, but he and Elic both shivered uncontrollably. Myn was wet up one side from foot to shoulder.

"What's happened now?" Stell asked.

"Myn almost fell through the ice," Elic said. "He's chilled through, but it could have been much worse. I thought we'd lost him. It's almost too strange to tell — an eagle swooped down and rescued him."

"An eagle? How ... interesting." She turned her attention to the shaking boy. Elic helped her peel Myn's wet clothes off. He had scratches on his shoulders where the eagle's talons had punctured his coat.

"I'm sure he tried to be careful," Stell murmured.

The door opened. "Who did?" Mam asked. She carried her healer's bag.

"Young Myn, here," Stell explained.

Mam examined the child and pronounced him cold but otherwise fine. She applied a salve to the scratches. Stell wrapped him in blankets and set him by the fire with a cup of warm milk.

Mam turned to Elic. "Here's the food you were going to take home," she said. "Jagree told me you got damp, too. I brought some dry clothes from the rag bag. I hope they still fit. Sorry I can't help with the boots."

"I have an old pair of my father's," Stell said. "They were too small for Crane, but they might fit you." She fetched them from her room. "Ketty borrowed them while she was here. I'm glad I hadn't packed them away yet."

Elic accepted the clothing and boots and went to Crane's room to change. His shirt was dry enough, but he had to change his long underwear, trousers, and socks. The dry trousers were threadbare and a little short in the leg. They would be adequate for Elic to get home. The boots fit well enough with dry socks. He didn't care that they were scuffed and worn.

When he came out, Old Myn had arrived. Mam was giving him a look that rivaled the eagle's glare.

"About time," she said.

Old Myn brushed past the women and went to his son. "He doesn't look so bad to me."

"No, he doesn't, thanks to Elic here," Mam said. "Where were you, I'd like to know? A six-year-old can't look after himself!"

"Now, Sudi, it could have been any of them," Stell said. "Remember how it was when we were small? We'll all have to keep a closer watch on the children now that the river is full again."

Mam gazed at Elic. "It's a good thing *somebody* was watching."

"It wasn't only me." He looked past his mother at Stell. She didn't say anything, but blushed and looked away as if to hide a secret smile.

Just then, Sunnea came in, carrying a bundle. "I brought dry clothes for Myn."

"Isn't that just like a man, to forget something so obvious?" Mam fumed.

"He was in a hurry to get to his boy," Sunnea said.

Old Myn had pulled a chair up next to his son and sat with his arm around him. Sunnea gave the bundle of clothes to Elic. Their eyes met, but he couldn't read the look she gave him. Before he could speak, she had turned and was out the door. He stared after her.

"Give me those!" Mayor Myn said. He grabbed the

bundle from Elic.

Mam reached for the clothes. "Allow me."

Myn pulled them away. "I think I can dress my own son."

"How about lunch?" Stell asked. "I've got a big pot of soup on that should be about ready."

Mam and Old Myn reached a grudging peace during the meal. By the time they finished eating, Young Myn was warm and able to tell about his ordeal. He made an epic of it, leaving nothing out. Elic wouldn't have trusted all the details, had he not seen it himself.

"You can have that story, if you want it," the boy told Stell at the conclusion.

"I'm not sure I could tell it half so well. I especially liked the part with the eagle."

"Well, I didn't!" Old Myn declared. "What kind of world is it, when an eagle plucks a child from the river like he was a fish?"

"It did save your son's life," Stell reminded him. "I'm sure it won't be a regular thing."

When Elic left the inn after lunch, he looked for the eagle. It was not on the roof or soaring above. Young Myn's rescue had amazed everyone who witnessed it. Only Stell had not acted surprised. Perhaps her old friend had come to call. If so, he was being as secretive as before.

Elic returned home, shaken by the anxious moment when he thought the boy was lost. He stuffed his wet boots with rags and set them by the fire, then hung his wet clothes on the line next to his damp chore trousers. He'd knocked the dried mud off and washed them. Not all of the stains had come out, but they would be fine for garden work and house chores.

Tired from the morning's excitement, Elic picked up Soorhi's diary and climbed into bed to read while he rested. He paged through to the next substantial entry. Years had passed, and Soorhi's eyesight must have worsened because the handwriting was a large, untidy scrawl with an inky fingerprint at the beginning of each line. At least now Elic knew why Soorhi's handwriting had always been hard to read.

Ersi gave me surprising news. He's getting married and won't be back in the fall. There's something about his wife that prevents them from living in the city. He wouldn't explain what it was. When he said that, I had a vision, though of the past, not the future: a tall village girl being mistreated. I couldn't see her clearly, but I saw Ersi, coming to her rescue. Neither of us is a young man anymore, so I'm happy for him. It's good to find love ... with an equal. I will miss him. I could always count on him to come and go like the seasons. Now, how will I know when it's spring?

So here was another loss, if under happier circumstances than some. Elic wondered about the mystery of Ersi's bride, though perhaps the diary would reveal more on that subject later. He inferred Dila was still at the school because Soorhi didn't mention her in the discussion of love, other than the fleeting reference to equals. If she had been gone, Soorhi might have felt free to express his feelings. He didn't write much of anything for another few years.

> I woke' this morning with a vision forming, the' most vivid and urge'nt I've' e've'r had. Ersi ne'e'ds me'. I must go to him, though I barely know whe're' he' is. I saw him in a swamp in the' de'se'rt, ne'ar an orchard. Doe's that e've'n make' se'nse'? He' said, "De'e'p Rive'r," which could be' the' name' of the' place'. It's be'e'n a long time' since' I trave'le'd, but if I must, I will. Ersi ne'e'ds me'.

Elic sat back with a thrill of anticipation. Here was the first mention of Deep River in the diary. Whenever Soorhi had traveled before, he had some kind of adventure. Maybe even Deep River could be exciting. There was also a sense of foreboding. His brother's need drew Soorhi to Deep River. But Elic had never met Ersi or heard him mentioned outside this diary. As far as he knew, Soorhi had always lived alone. Was it adventure he traveled toward or disaster? Elic turned the page and read on.

> Dila has pointe'd out that pe'rhaps trave'ling on foot is not the' be'st plan at my age'. She' found De'e'p

River on the map and worked out the best way to get there. I am to go by coach to Oxbow, then find someone to take me to Deep River from there. She has already paid for my seat, out of her own pocket, so I must travel in comfort for a change. How she spoils me! I thought she would be a society matron with a rich husband and several children by now, but she says that's not the life for her. The children are lucky to have her. She'll take good care of the school while I am away.

There followed an entry dated the next day, in Misty Pass.

I have completed the first leg of my journey. Travel by coach is a novel experience. I can't see well enough to enjoy the view out the window, but it was pleasant to sleep and travel at the same time. The trip was uneventful. I must admit the leave-taking was bittersweet. Dila walked me to the coach, and at the last moment, she offered to come with me. That was kind of her; she always thinks of others. As much as I wanted her company, I needed her to stay behind and take care of the school. She took it harder than I would have expected — she started to cry when she asked when I would be back. I couldn't tell her, since I don't know exactly why I'm going, only that I must go. She' said, "I was going to say I'd wait for you, but I gue's I already have'." I didn't understand her meaning until several hours later. Too late'. I should have' let her come' along.

"You should have told her how you felt twenty years ago," Elic muttered, echoing Stell's sentiment. How could an intelligent man be so foolish? He had visions, but he couldn't see what was right in front of him until it was too late. That was his real blindness.

The next entry brought him to Deep River, and Elic was eager to know what came next.

I found Ersi. It was just like' my vision — a swamp in a de'se'rt, ne'ar orchards. This is dry country, but fe'rtile'. The' rive'r allows the'm to grow just about anything. De'e'p Rive'r is the' sort of place' whe're' Pop would have' worke'd. Maybe' that's why Ersi se'ttle'd he're'. He' found an old camp in a swamp far outside' the' village' and fixe'd up a shack to live' in. He' e've'n plante'd a garde'n on highe'r ground. Whe'n I got the're', the' garde'n had run to we'e'ds and they we're' all down with a fe've'r — Ersi, his wife' Kirazik, and the'ir little' boy, poor fellow. What little' I could se'e' of he'r, Kirazik looks like' Bushy's siste'r, dark-skinne'd and probably tall, with straight, dark hair. Ersi let on he'r fathe'r was

Aklaka. Is that why they couldn't stay in the city? Why she was mistreated? It hardly matters now. They're both dead.

Elic almost closed the diary right there. It was too much pointless loss for one life. How would even Soorhi find the good in this? But he'd written, "They're *both* dead." There was a third person in that shack. Elic couldn't help himself. He turned the page and read on.

Ersi thought he was living in secret, but at least one person knew about him. At least, someone suspected there was illness here. A woman named Elika rode out, before I knew Ersi was dead. I met her at the plank bridge. My eyesight may be poor, but I saw the power in her. She's a real healer. She called me a seer, a fancy name for a person who sometimes dreams true. She didn't waste time. She recognized swamp fever, though it seemed more severe than usual. Perhaps Ersi and Kirazik were already weakened by something else. It was too late to save them, but she treated the little fellow. He'll probably have recurrences throughout his life. At least now we know what to take for it. She gave me a preventive dose, just in case. She puts the child at three years old; she has a daughter a bit younger. He's dark like his mother. He has Ersi's blue eyes. He watches me and doesn't say a word. Elika advised me to get him out of the swamp as soon as he's well, but the last thing Ersi told me was to keep him here, out of sight. I promised I would. Elika did not approve. She left us with netting, so at least the bugs won't eat us alive. I'm raising a child. That's my new life.

There was that refrain again. Elic had hoped Soorhi might see Dila again, but it seemed unlikely now. He was surprised to read his grandmother's name, though he shouldn't have been. She'd been Deep River's healer for a long time, from before Soorhi arrived. The little daughter Soorhi mentioned would have been Elic's mother. The thing that most caught Elic's attention was the description of the little fellow. As Stell had confirmed, he wasn't Soorhi's son, but he was close. And he had those blue eyes in an Aklaka face, as in Soorhi's long-ago vision. Like Stell's old friend.

Chapter 21. The Dance

Elic had never seen a person with dark skin and blue eyes. No surprise — he'd spent his whole life in Deep River, where practically everyone was related by blood, marriage, or both. Soorhi, who was widely traveled and knew a broader range of people, regarded the combination of features as rare enough to mention. There were plenty of blue eyes in Deep River, but Crane's had been the only dark face.

The similarity between Soorhi's little fellow and Stell's old friend nudged Elic to keep reading. Perhaps the mystery would be solved within the diary. He scanned quickly through several entries. Soorhi didn't write much or often in those days, busy as he was raising a small child. He kept his promise to his brother to hide the boy, but Elic's grandmother was their connection to the outside world. Elika's name appeared frequently, and sometimes that of Elic's mother, Sudi. She would have been very young then, not yet able to reveal secrets. Although Soorhi never said so directly, Elic sensed strong affection for Elika in the brief diary entries. He had at least one true friend in those difficult days.

Elic remembered Grammy Elika, though she had died when he was about six years old, before Jagree was born. She had healing power, sharp features, and a sharper tongue, which led some to call her a witch. He didn't know whether she used the word for herself. She didn't have much use for other people's opinions. What Elic remembered most was her kindness, especially to women and children, and most especially to him, at that time the only child of her only child. She had no patience with men who were not equally kind, a trait Mam had inherited. He could almost hear Elika's stinging words directed at someone, possibly Old Myn, the recipient of Mam's ire just today. Elika could be fond of men, too. Elic never knew Grampa Greelin, but by all accounts, Elika had loved him wholeheartedly. She had approved of Elic's father Ohme, too, and he adored her. She must have had similar affection for Soorhi, to help him in secret for so many years.

As much as it intrigued Elic to read Soorhi's impressions of Elika, he was most interested in the child.

My poor little fellow has no name. I'm sure Ersi

told me', but that day is a blur. The' boy stoppe'd speaking for wee'ks afte'r his pare'nts die'd. When he' found his voice' again, I aske'd him his name'. He' claime'd not to know. Pe'rhaps he' doe'sn't re'membe'r, e'ithe'r. I don't want to force' a name' of my choosing on him. The're' is still a chance' he' will re'membe'r or choose' a ne'w one' himse'lf.

What kind of parent let a child go nameless? But Soorhi had never been a parent. He was making it up as he went along. With only two of them in the house, maybe they didn't need names. And it explained why he kept referring to the child as "little fellow." Filled with curiosity about this odd household, Elic turned to the next entry.

What a mistake' that was! I should have' name'd the' boy whe'n I had the' chance'. Now he' choose's a ne'w name' e've'ry day, and some'time's more' than one'. I have' to use' the' name', or he' lose's his te'mpe'r, and it's a hot one' for such a little' fe'llow. If I'm lucky, he' make's up a short name' — "Ee" or "Bup" — or take's an animal name', like' Frog. Today he' strung toge'the'r so many syllable's he' ran out of bre'ath. It was too much for me' to re'membe'r. Lucky for me', he' couldn't, e'ithe'r.

Elic chuckled about that. It sounded like Soorhi got

what he deserved and learned a lesson. The subject came up several times, usually no more than a record of a funny or unusual name. The next longish entry was dated several years into Soorhi's time in the swamp.

> *By Elika's calculation, my little fellow is about seven years old now, and a good student. He reads and writes with ease already. And he can draw. He practices his writing on the wall, so as not to waste the paper Elika brings us. He covers every sheet with pictures of ducks, herons, and cranes. He is growing long-legged, and I tease him that he will turn into a wading bird. I can see the pictures only up close in strong light, but I'm saving them. He has a real talent, and maybe not just for art. I have a feeling about him, much like I had with Ordy.*

Elic's stomach flipped with a little thrill. Had Soorhi found another wizard in the making, this time in his own family? There was no Dillum to take him to for training, and not even spell books to study, the way Crane had. At least Elic now knew where the stack of drawings had come from, and the one on Crane's wall. He wished he could tell Crane they were drawn by a wizard-to-be.

The next entry was dated soon after, and Elic read on, obsessed now with the unfolding story.

> *I asked the little fellow his name today, and when he told me, I felt a chill. I had to ask him how to*

spell it, and even the letters made me uneasy. I don't know why. I've never heard the name before, and I don't know what it might mean. Did I have a vision about it? I asked him to change it, but he got angry and wrote it seven times on the wall of the shack: Yrae Yrae Yrae Yrae Yrae Yrae Yrae. When I close my eyes, that's all I see. I hope he changes it soon.

Elic dropped the diary as if it were on fire. Had he read that right? Soorhi's little fellow was Yrae, the Mad Wizard? And he looked like ... which meant that ...

What did it mean?

As he bent to pick up the book, someone knocked at the door. He went to answer it, trying to puzzle out the connections. Had Stell lied, or did she not know? What about Crane?

He opened the door to find Sunnea standing there. His thoughts scattered.

Before he could even greet her, she thrust a bundle into his hands. "Get your things on and let's go!"

"What?" He gazed at her with distracted pleasure. She wore her blue cape with the fur-lined hood over her best dress, with dainty gloves and incongruously heavy boots.

"Get dressed, then coat, hat, gloves!"

"But where are we going?" Elic was baffled, though pleased she hadn't come to fight.

"Do you want an adventure or not? Let's go!"

It appeared she wouldn't answer him until he agreed

to come along. By now, his curiosity was piqued. And he liked this mood she was in — direct and in charge, but also mischievous. Her eyes shone with excitement, and her cheeks were pink under her hood.

"I would be pleased to join you, but I can't go out in public dressed like this." Elic indicated his ill-fitting, worn-out trousers. "And everything else is wet."

"I thought of that." She poked the bundle in his hands. "I swiped these from my father's workshop. They should fit."

Out of excuses, Elic hung his quilt over the wash line and ducked behind it to change. He removed his shabby trousers, leaving the long underwear — the night was chilly enough for that. He donned his best shirt, worn only briefly for the disastrous betrothal supper. He unfolded the new trousers Sunnea had stolen for him. They were a fine, dark gray wool, much nicer than anything he had ever worn. He pulled them on.

"How do they fit?" Sunnea called from the other side of the quilt.

"Like they were made for me."

She laughed. "They were. Your mother ordered your wedding suit when you were away with Crane, as a surprise. Papa finished the stitching before the curse was lifted, but ... well, you know."

Elic knew all too well. He chose not to comment and risk spoiling whatever this was. He pulled on the matching overtunic and adjusted the ties on the sides. It had intricate embroidery around the hem, arm openings, and neck, summer blue against the stormy gray. The scuffed old boots detracted from the fine outfit, but the weather still called for them.

Sunnea smiled when he came out from behind the quilt. "That turned out well."

"Me, or the suit?"

"Hm!" was all her answer.

Elic wrapped the knitted scarf around his neck, then pulled on his coat, hat, and gloves. "There, I'm ready. But I haven't eaten yet. I was going to have supper at the Heron."

"There'll be food when we get there," Sunnea assured him. She tugged at his scarf. "This ugly thing was the first knitting I ever finished."

"It keeps my neck warm," Elic said.

"I could make a better one now." Sunnea displayed a lacy glove. "I finished one of these just in time for the weather to warm up last spring, and the other today."

"Pretty," Elic said. "But are they warm?"

"Warm enough." She grabbed his hand and led him out to the road, where a pony and cart waited. "Tiek lent me her cart. She and Breff and Kiat went ahead in his buggy."

Near the cart, Elic froze in his tracks. The silver apple blossoms would look lovely pinned to Sunnea's best dress. He half turned back but stopped again. He didn't know yet where they stood. A gift now might seem pushy.

"What now?" she asked.

"Nothing." Elic helped her onto the seat of the open cart, then climbed up beside her. She took the reins and clucked to the pony, which started off at a trot.

"Am I right to guess we're going to the dance in Bitter Springs?" he asked.

"Maybe." She tossed him a quick, winking smile.

"I thought you were going with Huvro. Or was it Rovhi?"

"You were wrong, then." She shook her head. "What made you think that?"

"I overheard you talking to them about the dance, that day by the river. You said you'd see them there."

"I'm sure we'll see lots of people. Besides, they're my friends, and yours too, Elic. I've known them a long time."

"And how long have you known me?"

She glanced at him. "All my life."

She had a point. It wasn't as if he had refrained from talking to other women. It wouldn't do to mention Kiat now; that would start a fight for sure, the last thing he wanted when Sunnea finally seemed willing to give him another chance.

"I appreciate you riding with me," Sunnea said. "I knew Papa and Mother wouldn't want me to go alone. I told them you were taking me so I wouldn't have to ride with them."

That wasn't quite the reason Elic was hoping for, but he chuckled at her little deception. It was the sort of thing Dila would have done. Soorhi would approve. They rolled out of the village and into the dark countryside. The sun had set, and the waning moon had not yet risen. The stars were blocked by patchy clouds. The cart's lantern cast a pool of light onto the dark road. In the distance, Elic could make out the light on another vehicle.

"This is a strange adventure," he said. "We can't even see where we're going."

"Should I turn back?" she asked.

"No, as long as you know the way."

"Papa says there are signs."

"It's cold tonight," Elic fretted. "Is it far? Are you dressed warmly enough?"

"Trust me, will you?"

"I'm sorry," he said. "I guess I worry about the cold after what happened with Myn."

"That's why I'm with you now. When I saw the way you took care of him ..." Sunnea shook her head and urged the pony to a quicker pace. "Don't worry, we'll be there before you know it."

It wasn't quite that fast, but the pony was strong and eager, and Sunnea was right — when they reached the main road, signs pointed left toward Oxbow, right toward Bitter Springs and Stony Creek, and back the way they'd come, toward Deep River. A sign pointing to Deep River had stood all through the years of Yrae's Curse, but no outsider had been able to follow its direction. Elic shivered. That was a powerful curse for a little fellow.

They turned right and drove straight until they reached another sign directing them left. They came in sight of Bitter Springs soon after. Elic leaned forward to take it all in. The village wasn't much larger than Deep River but had an aura of wonder because it was his first sight of any other village. Tonight, the town was packed with visitors, all streaming toward the Village Hall in the center of town.

"Where do we leave the cart?" Elic asked.

As if in answer, a boy dashed up. "There's stabling around back of the Hall, if you'll follow me." He stroked the pony's nose, reminding Elic of Jagree. He led them to a large temporary shelter that had been erected for visitors' animals. It appeared all the boys not interested in dancing had volunteered as grooms. Tiek's pony would be well cared for.

Sunnea tugged off her boots and slipped into shoes. Elic hadn't thought of that. She took his arm, and they walked around to the front. The Hall was bright, noisy, and warm, packed with people all talking at once. At first, Elic didn't recognize anyone, a peculiar experience after a lifetime of knowing everyone he saw. Then he began to pick out familiar faces and caught sight of the musicians he had met at the Blue Heron, playing fiddle, flute, and drums on a small stage. The floor had been cleared; chairs lined the walls. He stared at the long tables laden with food that took up one end of the Hall. Sunnea gazed longingly at the dance floor.

"You don't have to stay with me, if you'd rather not," he said.

"No, it's fine. We can dance after you eat."

"I'll try," he promised, though he wasn't sure. Some of the couples already out on the floor made it look easy, but there were as many others stumbling over each other.

Elic filled a plate with sliced meat, cheese, bread, and an apple, and accepted a glass of sweet cider. He found two chairs together and sat down with Sunnea. She hadn't taken anything except cider. She stole a piece of cheese and some bread from his plate.

"You shouldn't eat alone." She grinned as she took a bite.

While they ate, Elic studied the crowd. Most of Deep River had traveled to Bitter Springs this night. Mam and Pap twirled past, laughing and more graceful than he would have expected. In the far corner, children danced with each other. Elic smiled as Briato picked up Brynnit and danced away with his youngest child in his arms.

With a full stomach, Elic was more willing to consider dancing. They joined a circle dance that involved stepping in one direction and then clapping hands — simple enough for even the smallest children, though Elic wished he'd worn more graceful footwear. Once he was used to moving to the music, it was easier to get the feel of the partner dances. They mostly consisted of a few steps, repeated over and over. He had to count out loud at first but soon forgot to in his enjoyment. Sunnea talked him into trying a dance that turned out to be fast and complicated, and left him sweating and out of breath. He was wearing too many layers but didn't mind — Sunnea was smiling at him.

He sat down to rest while she continued dancing, first with her father, then with Huvro, then with somebody he'd never seen before. Jealousy bubbled up, until she turned and met his gaze from all the way across the room. She hadn't forgotten him. Her whole face was alight, she was laughing and enjoying herself, and he was somehow part of that.

Kiat flopped down next to him, her face red with exertion. "Phew!" she puffed. "So you decided to come after all! And dressed better than any man here."

"Not my decision," he said. "Sunnea dragged me along with her and provided the suit."

Kiat chuckled. "I'm glad to hear it. Having a good time?"

"Better than I expected. Would you care to dance?"

"I'd love to!"

Elic didn't know a lot about dancing, but it seemed that Kiat was a less skilled dancer than Sunnea, though no worse than he was. They laughed and stumbled their way through two songs. Then Elic danced with his mother.

"You should ask Ati to dance," Mam said. "She's been sitting there almost since they arrived. I'm not sure she's even danced with Yshna."

"Why do you think she'd want to dance with me, then?"

"She might not want to, but it would be thoughtful to ask. It never hurts to be on good terms with your future mother-in-law."

The song ended before he could argue. Mam made a graceful bow and turned to dance with Toli. Without much enthusiasm, Elic approached Sunnea's stepmother.

"Good evening, Ati. Would you like to dance?"

She stared up at him. "Unlike some people, I am not here to make a fool of myself." She gazed past him. He turned and saw Yshna dancing with Keena. They were both laughing, but he couldn't see anything particularly foolish in their behavior. "He thinks he's still twenty," Ati muttered. "It's up to me to make sure Sunnea behaves properly."

"That's very ... dutiful of you," Elic said. "But I'm sure you have nothing to worry about."

"Maybe you do." Again, he followed her gaze, this time to where Sunnea stood talking with Huvro, Rovhi, and Kiat. Tiek and Breff were also part of the group, each holding one of their infant twins. Mynna and Brak joined them while Elic watched. He didn't see anything amiss — just a crowd of old friends, enjoying a festive evening. Sunnea gave him such a radiant smile he could hardly see anything else. No, for the first time in days, he couldn't find anything to worry about.

Ati must have seen the smile, too. "As for that dance …" Her expression softened. "Ask me again the next time you wear that suit."

Although she didn't say *at your wedding*, Elic was sure that's what she meant. He could almost believe in that event again. He nodded politely and approached the group of friends. Before he had taken two steps, Brynnit, Silib, and Ylani joined hands and circled him.

"Help!" he cried. "I'm surrounded by little girls! What'll I do?"

They giggled. "Dance with us, Teacher!"

He gave in to their pleas and twirled comically at the center of their circle. When they reached Sunnea's group, Breff passed his baby to a startled Sunnea and took Elic's place, spinning away with the squealing children. The rest of the group welcomed Elic to join them. After all, they were his friends, too.

Sunnea laughed as she held the baby uncertainly. "What do I do?" she asked, as the child twisted to stare at Elic.

"He can almost hold up his head, but you need to support him, like this." Tiek demonstrated with her twin. Sunnea cuddled the baby closer, her hand behind his head, and gave Elic an embarrassed smile.

"We'll have one of our own next summer," Mynna confided. Brak put his arm around her and smiled fondly. She smiled back, a look that was not at all haughty.

"Congratulations," Elic said. "I learned only recently you had married. Your father didn't seem too pleased."

"When does he ever? I worry about my brother, but I couldn't stay in that house." She looked straight at Elic. "Maybe Papa will do better after today, though."

His face heated. "Oh, you heard about that?"

"Everyone heard. What if you hadn't been there? Young Myn would have been swept away."

Rather than explain the eagle's role, Elic held out his hand to Sunnea. "Another dance?"

She passed the baby to Kiat and took his hand. He whirled her out of the circle, and they danced the next three songs together.

"Having a good time?" she asked.

"Yes. Better than Ati, anyway."

She laughed at that. "She thinks she has to watch me every moment! We should leave so she can enjoy herself."

"Already?" The party was still going strong. He hadn't seen anyone else leave yet, not even parents with small children.

Sunnea didn't answer. She led the way to collect their wraps. He didn't mind too much. The dancing was fun, but he had a blister on one heel, and his legs were starting to ache. They stepped outside. The darkness seemed darker after the glare of lamplight. It was a shock to step out of the steamy Hall into the frosty night.

"It feels good to cool off, doesn't it?" Sunnea asked.

It was a relief, at least at first. When they reached the stable, at least four boys offered to hitch up the pony. Somehow, the job got done, and they took their places on the seat again. Sunnea put her boots back on and picked up the reins. As they rolled away from Bitter Springs, she sighed happily.

"Thank you for coming with me, Elic," she said.

"You're welcome. Thank you for making me come. I'm glad I didn't miss it."

"The musicians were good, weren't they?"

"They made it easy to dance. We should reinstate the summer dance in Deep River."

She elbowed him playfully. "Will that be your first act as mayor?"

He laughed but didn't say anything. It looked like he would have to live with that crazy idea forever.

"I'm not joking," she said. "You'd be a good mayor. People listen to you."

He considered that. If Sunnea believed in him, maybe it wasn't so crazy.

Chapter 22. The Talk

Elic and Sunnea rode in silence, the only sound the clop of the pony's hooves on the frozen road. The sky had cleared. Under the frosty starlight, it felt colder than before. Elic shivered and moved closer to Sunnea.

"When I said I brought you along to avoid riding with my parents," she said, "I wasn't entirely truthful." Hope warmed him, but before he could speak, she continued. "I thought if I could get you away from Deep River, it might be easier."

"What might be easier?"

"To talk, about … everything."

"I've been trying. You said you were tired of hearing it."

"I know," she said. "I thought I was. But I should know what you went through. I don't want you to lose your mind again."

"I didn't!" he objected. "Not quite. It was terrible, knowing about the curse, and forced by the curse to keep silent; knowing what was possible, unable to say anything …"

"Now you can."

"I always say the wrong thing."

"But you usually *do* the right thing." Sunnea gave him an encouraging smile. "So, talk. I'll try to listen this time."

He took his time, gathering his thoughts before he spoke. It meant a great deal to have this chance to explain. He didn't want to waste it, though he could hardly make things worse.

"I didn't expect it to be like this, when the curse was broken," he said at last. "I thought everything would be … clear. Maybe I should have known better, after what I experienced with Crane. It took real effort to escape the curse. We had to push through it, and I almost gave up. Crane was stronger and kept going. I followed him. When we broke through, the freedom hit us so hard, neither of us could stand up." As he spoke of the experience, he felt again an echo of that dizzying release. "I had never felt so alive."

"Then why did you come back?" It was the same question as before, curious now, not angry.

"You really don't know?" he asked. "I came home for

you."

"Oh," she whispered. She didn't say anything more for a long time. "It's my fault you suffered so much under the curse."

"No, it's Yrae's fault. I know you tried to help me. I didn't repay you very well after the curse was lifted. I did everything I could to drive you away."

"You almost succeeded," Sunnea said, a tremor in her voice. Was she angry?

"Only *almost*? That's something, then. I couldn't blame you for wanting to break with me when I was such a fool. How could I believe I loved you only because of Yrae's Curse?"

"What does Yrae know of love?" she muttered.

For a fleeting moment, he thought of Stell's old friend, and of Soorhi, giving up his life in the city to live in a swamp and raise his little fellow. But sharing these guesses with Sunnea could wait.

"When I was a child, before the curse could touch me, I already adored you," he said. "How could I forget that? When I escaped the curse, my first thought was of you. I wanted us both to know that freedom, together. Even Yrae couldn't change that. But ..."

"But, what?" Sunnea asked. "Your wish came true. We are free of the curse — all of us."

"I didn't know it would change things. Between us."

"Neither did I," she whispered. "But when it lifted, my first thought was also of you."

Elic remembered now how she had come to him early that morning, just after Crane's departure, and how the sight of her had lifted his spirits.

"And yet, I wanted to escape, to fly away," Sunnea

continued.

"I did, too. Maybe just because it was possible," Elic said. "Where did you want to go? And what would you do there?"

"I don't know. Anywhere!" Sunnea laughed at the notion. "Maybe I could go somewhere else and work as a dressmaker. I don't love it like Papa does, but I'm not bad. I do enjoy embroidery."

Elic thought of the summer-blue pattern decorating his overtunic. "You did a nice job on my suit."

"I finished it this morning." She sighed. "Every time I imagined leaving Deep River ... I wasn't alone. You were with me."

"And you wanted that?"

"Since I was a little girl, I dreamed of being married and having my own home, my own children. For a long time, I dreamed of being married to *you* and having *your* children. I wanted at least two."

"Two is a nice number," Elic said, thinking of growing up with Jagree.

"For me it was more than *nice*," Sunnea said. "Mama promised me a little brother or sister and let me feel the baby move. But it all went wrong. Not only didn't I get my brother, I lost Mama, too. Child me must have wanted to fix that somehow." She sighed. "I didn't know any details at the time, but while I was spending so much time with your mother caring for you, she told me what happened. The baby died in the womb. Mama was afraid of magic, so Elika and Sudi did everything else they knew to start labor so they could deliver the body. Nothing worked. By the time Mama agreed to let Elika use magic, she was gravely ill. They couldn't save her."

"I'm sorry," Elic said. "I didn't know all of that either."

"After the curse lifted ... I don't know. I no longer wanted to marry for the sake of being married. I couldn't imagine *belonging* to anyone."

He stared at her in surprise. "Is that how you see it?"

"Doesn't everyone?"

He'd never thought about it that way. With chagrin, he realized he'd been wanting a wife as cook, laundress, and bedwarmer, without considering how she might feel about it, or what he might do for her. Maybe he could offer to cook her a meal. What about other couples? Mam and Pap didn't act that way, but they were unusual for many reasons. "So you think Ati *belongs* to your father?"

She snorted at that, then laughed out loud. "No, you're right." She wiped her eyes. "If anything, he belongs to her."

"Maybe we can try again, and do things our own way," Elic said. He thought of Soorhi again, and of Stell's advice. Soorhi had missed his chance. It was not too late for Elic to take it. He drew a deep breath. "You probably deserve better than me. For what it's worth, I love you, Sunnea. More than ever. I understand if you don't want to risk your life to give me children, but ..."

"I might consider it for you," she said. "What do you think of the name Sulika for a girl?"

Elic hid his surprise. "Too pretty not to use," he said. "And maybe Crane for a boy." He put his arm around Sunnea and hugged her close. He no longer cared what was proper. He leaned down and gave her a quick kiss on the lips. He half expected her to slap him, but it was worth it.

She stopped the cart, dropped the reins, and grabbed his shoulders with both hands. He was completely unprepared for the kiss she gave him, longer than he would have imagined possible, though he was sorry when it ended. His heart raced and his insides thrilled with excitement. She released him and picked up the reins again. They started forward at a walk. Neither spoke for a long time.

She exhaled a long sigh. "I've been wanting to do that for so long."

"You didn't have to bring me all the way out here for that," he teased. "We could have kissed at home."

"Could we?"

Maybe she was right. Even without the curse, they had continued to live with old habits. Look how long it had taken just to leave town. Too bad it was so cold — there were probably all kinds of things they could get away with out here in the dark, away from prying eyes.

"I always admired you," Sunnea said. "When we were young, the other children all listened to you. Then, when you started teaching, you had such a way with the students. And the way you took care of Myn today ..."

"I'm nothing special."

"You are! Can't you see? It doesn't take magic, or, or ..."

He heard the tremor in her voice again, and a tightness, as if her jaw was clenched. She was angry, and he had no idea why. She stopped the cart again. Elic couldn't see a reason — he didn't even know where they were.

But when she spoke, it was to the pony. "What's

wrong, Brownie? Elic, why did he stop?"

Elic remembered Jagree's comment about the cold freezing the breath in a horse's nostrils. Was that true? He climbed down to check. The pony's muzzle was frosted with ice, and his head hung as he tried to draw breath.

"I wish Jagree were here," Elic murmured. "He'd know what to do." He needed something warm, but what? He pulled off a glove and laid his hand first over one nostril, then the other, until the ice thawed. The pony snorted and tossed his head, ready to go again.

Elic pulled his glove on and climbed back up. "It's getting colder. Let's go."

Sunnea snapped the reins clumsily and the pony broke into a trot. Sunnea shivered next to him, but they would soon be home.

"Will ... you ... drive?" she asked through clenched teeth. "I ... can't ... feel my ... fingers."

Elic looked at her in alarm. In the light of the lantern, her face seemed to have no color. He pulled off his scarf and wrapped it around Sunnea's neck, under her hood. He took the reins in one hand and slipped the other arm around her shoulders. She tucked her hands under her cloak and leaned against him, shivering uncontrollably.

"You didn't dress warmly enough, did you?"

"It wasn't this cold when I was getting ready. I knew it would be warm at the Hall, and how could I dance in stiff, itchy flannels?"

He wasn't sure how long the trip home should take, nor how far they had already come, but it seemed too long. An icy wind had risen, blowing in from Sunnea's side of the cart. "Do you want to switch places?"

She shook her head. "I'm ... fine. Just drive."

Elic had never driven much, but the pony knew the way. Elic paid enough attention to keep them on the road. Most of his mind was on Sunnea. As a light from Deep River appeared ahead of them, she stopped shivering.

"Ahh, now I feel warmer," she mumbled.

It wasn't any warmer. If anything, it had gotten steadily colder as they drove. Elic knew he needed to get her into a warm room, now. But as far as he knew, they had been the first to leave the dance. Everyone from Deep River was still in Bitter Springs. Whose house would be warm?

"We're going to the Heron," he announced. "We'll be there soon."

"Ati says I'm not supposed to go in there," she murmured.

"You visited Crane. You brought Young Myn's clothes."

"That was ... during the day." Her words, barely audible, slurred together.

Elic held her tightly and urged the pony to a faster trot. "Then it'll be an adventure."

Chapter 23. Warming Up

After what seemed like forever, the cart rattled up to the inn. Elic jumped down and looped the reins around the hitching post, then lifted Sunnea down from the seat. When he set her on her feet, she collapsed against him. He carried her inside and shouldered the door closed behind them. The common room was dim, warmed by a low fire. Stell was nowhere to be seen. Elic heard muffled voices from somewhere but couldn't make out the words.

"Auntie Stell!" he shouted. "Come quickly, I need

your help!"

She came out of her room with a lamp in her hand, smoothing down her hair and straightening her dress. "What is it?" Before he could answer, she saw Sunnea, limp in his arms. "Another frozen friend in need of thawing?" Her worried expression belied her light tone. She pulled a high-backed bench near the fire and had him set Sunnea there. "Elic, build the fire up," she instructed. She took Sunnea's cloak and draped a warm shawl over her. "I don't suppose Sudi's at home?"

Elic shook his head. "She was still dancing when we left."

"Then it's up to you and me. I'll heat some soup — a few of us had a late supper, so it shouldn't take long. That'll warm her from the inside."

"So she'll be all right?" Elic stirred the fire and added more wood. "If I'd known the weather was going to turn like that, I would have insisted we stay in Bitter Springs. Even the pony —" He broke off. "I left the pony standing in the cold."

"I'll wake Jagree," Stell said from the kitchen. "He's in Crane's room — I didn't want him to be home all alone."

"I'll get him," Elic offered.

"No. Once you finish with the fire, get under that shawl with Sunnea. She needs your heat, too."

The fire was roaring now. Elic threw off his coat and sat close to Sunnea with the shawl over both of them. She was more alert, and shivering again, her arms folded tight against her chest. He gently unfolded them and pulled off her thin gloves. Her fingers felt like icicles and the nails had a bluish tinge.

"Warm your hands by the fire," he said. "They're near frozen."

With aching slowness, she stretched her arms out toward the blaze. She leaned closer and closer. "Stop!" Elic pulled her back before she put her hands into the flames.

"I can't feel the fire!" Her teeth chattered so hard, he could barely understand her.

"Hush, it's all right," he whispered. He took her hands between his and rubbed, but it didn't seem to do much good. What had Stell said? *She needs your heat.*

He lifted his tunic, shirt, and undershirt. "Put your hands under here." He gasped at the icy touch of her fingers on his chest but didn't pull away. He held her close and willed his warmth into her. After what seemed like hours, her hands weren't as cold against his skin. "Can you feel your fingers yet?"

"They hurt."

He knew what that meant. The blood was returning, a necessary but painful thing. Tears trickled from her eyes. She didn't sob or even whimper. He sympathized with her discomfort, but this show of bravery moved him even more. He pressed his mouth to hers. At first her lips felt cold and stiff. As they warmed, she responded with urgent passion. Her cold hands clung to his chest as she pulled him closer.

"That's the way to heat things up!" Stell commented. Elic and Sunnea broke apart. "See, you've brought the color back to her face." She didn't mention it, but he knew his own face was burning.

Stell gave him a steaming bowl of soup. When Sunnea started to pull her hands out, he shook his head.

"Leave them there. I'll feed you."

It was awkward, and strangely intimate, to feed her soup while she had her hands under his shirt. She kept her elbows down, out of his way, and opened her mouth like a baby bird. He held the bowl under her chin and spooned the warm soup in.

"They're a good team," Stell remarked to Jagree as she sent him out the door.

By the time Sunnea had eaten most of the bowl of soup, she had stopped shivering. Her hands now burned hot against Elic's skin, and when she pulled them out at last, they were red and swollen. She rubbed and scratched them.

"Now they itch," she said.

"Like when I nearly froze my feet off."

She smiled. "I remember that."

"You do? It was a long time ago."

"I know. I hid by the window and watched you write that message in the snow. I waited to show myself until you'd finished. I was so angry you'd misspelled my name, I wouldn't let you see me. When I heard what happened because you'd stayed out so long, I felt too guilty to tell anyone."

"I wouldn't misspell your name now," he whispered, and kissed her forehead, her nose, and both cheeks.

"I'm worried about the others."

"Which others?" Elic asked. His whole world was here.

"Everyone at the dance. Most people went in open carts. They might not be any more prepared for the cold than I was."

Elic hadn't given a thought to anyone else since

they'd left the dance, and now he was giddy with kissing and relief. But she was right. Several families had taken children and elders to Bitter Springs. What would they do if they got halfway home and started to freeze?

"Now I really wish Crane was here to fix the weather."

"Yes, that would be good," Stell agreed. "I wonder ..." She took the empty soup bowl and left the room.

Elic put his arm around Sunnea. She leaned her head against his chest. Had Stell gone outside for a quick look at the weather? He didn't hear a door open. Again, voices whispered in her room.

A moment later, she was back. "What do you know? There's a warm wind blowing."

Elic could hardly believe it, but soon Jagree came in and confirmed the news. "When I took the pony to the stable, it was freezing out. Now it's almost balmy. Is some wizard playing with our weather?"

Nobody answered him, but Elic turned and met Stell's gaze from across the room. She stared back at him for a moment, then retreated into the kitchen. Jagree went back to bed. Sunnea, warm now, dozed by the fire. Elic removed his arm from her shoulders and rose quietly. He rolled up his coat for a pillow and laid her down on the bench with the shawl over her. He joined Stell in the kitchen. She stood in front of the brick oven, her back to him.

"Do you have a guest tonight?" Elic asked. "An old friend, perhaps? Or someone who can become an eagle?"

She stiffened but didn't speak. After a moment, she nodded. "Can't it be both?" she whispered. She turned to face him.

"The same one as before?" Again, she nodded. "Jagree described him to me — a tall, dark-skinned man with deep blue eyes."

"So?" Her voice sounded bold, but her eyes looked worried.

"In his diary, Soorhi describes a person with those features, more than once. The first time, he had a vision of a young man who looked like that, left alone in a valley by a lot of Mountain Folk." Stell's eyes widened, but she didn't interrupt. "Later, he wrote about his own nephew, just a little boy, displaying those same features. A little boy who, when he was seven years old, called himself Yrae."

"Stop!" Stell raised her hand as if to fend off a blow. Shaking, she pulled out a chair and sank into it. She went on in a quieter voice. "Yes, my ... *friend* is Soorhi's nephew. I didn't know until recently. But there is no Yrae. Not anymore." Tears ran down her cheeks, but she stared at Elic with challenge in her eyes.

Her show of emotion unnerved Elic. "I'm ... glad to hear it." He didn't like looking down at her. He pulled out another chair and sat. "But if he isn't Yrae, who is he?"

"From before the time he left Soorhi until he met me, he called himself The Crane."

Elic started. He had suspected, but this statement revealed more about Stell's friend than he'd expected her to admit. "And after that?"

"He ... wasn't in his right mind. He went to the mountains, to be alone. But he's not Yrae. He's not!"

"You mean he's not *anymore*." She didn't contradict him. "And he's more than a friend, isn't he? He left one of his names with his son."

"I didn't leave it," said a deep, clear voice behind him. "She took it."

Stell laid a hand to her chest. Elic leaped from his seat and stared. A man stood in the shadowy doorway. He was nearly as tall as Crane, with a curly mane of graying hair and a shaggy beard. His eyes glittered in the lamplight. Were they blue? Elic couldn't tell in this light. He couldn't imagine them otherwise.

Stell regained her composure more quickly than Elic. She rose and stepped to the man's side, taking his arm. "Elic, this is Crane's father." She had tears in her eyes, but she looked relieved. She had carried that secret a long time. "Knot, this is Crane's oldest friend, Elic."

"So good to meet you," the man called Knot said. "Crane spoke of you often." He hesitated, then held out his hand.

"I'm sorry I can't say the same." After a moment, Elic took the offered hand and shook it. "But you finally came back to Stell. For her sake, I'm glad. But Auntie Stell, do you think it's a good idea for the wizard who cursed us to be in Deep River?"

"It wasn't a curse," they said together, and smiled at each other. "It was an enchantment," Knot continued.

"I don't see much difference," Elic said. "He shouldn't be here."

"No one will know!" Stell said. "We're very discreet."

In the other room, Sunnea sighed. Knot stiffened. Elic expected her to sit up and ask what they were talking about, but she didn't wake. After a moment, they continued speaking in whispers.

"I figured it out," Elic countered.

"You asked questions. You had clues," Stell replied. "No one else has read Soorhi's diary."

"You have my uncle's diary?" Knot broke in, speaking louder in his eagerness.

"Shh," Stell cautioned. "I'm going to borrow it when Elic's finished. You can see it then."

"I'm not sure I feel safe with him here," Elic said.

"I worry more about his safety," she said. Knot shook his head and smiled, but Stell continued. "Now that the enchantment is lifted, anyone could start asking questions, and they might not be as friendly as Elic."

"What could any of us do to the Mad Wizard?" Elic asked.

Knot frowned. Neither he nor Stell answered the question. "Deep River is in no danger," she said.

Elic thought about pressing the matter but chose to trust her word, at least for now. She was a good judge of character, and whatever name the man was using, it was clear she loved him. "Thank you for working our weather," Elic said at last.

"You're welcome," the wizard replied.

"Please keep our secret," Stell said. "Even from Sunnea." She looked Elic in the eye with an expression of such pleading that he had no choice. He nodded his assent.

The sounds of voices, rattling wheels, and creaking harness interrupted them. The populace of Deep River had returned from the dance. Knot and Stell exchanged a look, and he melted into the shadows of her room.

Elic remained where he was for a moment. He stared at his hand, unsure which was harder to believe — that he'd just shaken the hand of Yrae, or that he'd finally met

Crane's father. Sunnea sighed again, and he shook himself. "I'd better take her home."

"You two looked like you'd come to a new agreement," Stell said, with a wink and a smile.

"I guess we have," Elic said. "I should have thanked your friend for that, too."

"I'm not sure he had anything to do with it," she said.

"He kept you home tonight," Elic replied. "That gave us a warm refuge, and another chance."

Stell glanced toward Sunnea. "After *she* gave *you* another chance."

"I have enough thanks to spread around to all of you," Elic said.

Chapter 24. A New Beginning

Elic gazed at Sunnea, asleep on the bench in front of the fire. She lay on her side, her head cushioned on his rolled-up coat. He had never watched her sleep before. He hated to wake her when she looked so warm and peaceful. He stroked her hair and kissed her cheek.

"It's time to go home," he whispered.

She blinked drowsily. "Aren't we home?" she murmured, yawning. "No, I guess I was dreaming."

She sat up, stretched, and smiled at him in a way that made his skin tingle. He shook out his coat and put it on.

Stell had hung Sunnea's cloak by the door. Elic brought it to her and draped it around her shoulders. "How do you feel? Warm enough?"

"Yes, I'm fine."

As Elic opened the door to go out, Stell came out of her room. "Good night, you two."

"Good night, Auntie Stell," Elic said. "Thanks for everything."

They stepped outside and he closed the door behind them. The night was much warmer than when they had arrived — almost springlike, in fact. Clouds gathered and blotted out the stars. Rain seemed more likely than snow. The road had turned muddy from melting ice, and the river whispered its song again.

"How did the weather change so quickly?" Sunnea asked. "Earlier tonight, I nearly froze, and now I barely need my cloak."

"There's no explaining the weather, especially early in the season." Elic hoped she would accept his explanation and let the subject go. He didn't want to lie to her.

When they reached her house, they found it dark and empty. The embers of a banked fire glowed dully through the ashes.

"I could wait with you for Yshna and Ati," Elic offered.

"There's no need. I don't mean to sit up — I'm going straight to my warm bed."

"That sounds inviting," Elic whispered.

"Ati would not approve," Sunnea replied, a mischievous twinkle in her eye. "You'll have to take this with you."

She gave him a goodnight kiss he would never forget, not even if he lived as long as Soorhi. He floated home, warm all over. He barely noticed the mud and slush underfoot. Several wagons and buggies passed him on the way, carrying people laughing and talking about the dance. Their happy voices brought back to him all that had happened that night between him and Sunnea. They hadn't said as much in words, but new promises had been made, he was sure of it. When he got home, he stirred the fire and lit the lamp so he could find something important he'd put away. After a short search, he found the betrothal ring on the shelf with his shaving things, and the silver flower pin next to it. He stood close to his shaving glass to reinsert the earring. It took a few pokes to find the hole in his left earlobe. It had not closed. Once in place, the ring looked and felt as if it had never been removed.

It was late, Elic had been dancing, and he had a full day ahead of him. He knew he should go to bed. But he was too excited to sleep. He opened Soorhi's diary one more time.

> *This morning, I told my little fellow he looked like a long-legged crane. He laughed and said, "That's my name from now on." I think this time he means it. He wiped that awful name from the wall. May we never hear it again.*

If Stell hadn't told him, Elic would have been sure now. Soorhi's little fellow, Crane's father, and the Mad Wizard were all one. At least Soorhi was right on one count — the boy had kept the name Crane for years. But it wasn't the end of the name Yrae. Did Soorhi remember that name in later years, when Stell told frightening tales of the Mad Wizard? If he did, what a heavy load to bear. Rather than dwell on that, Elic turned to the next entry, dated three years later.

I have no doubt now — my little Crane-boy has great power. I can't teach him to use it, so I asked Elika if she had contact with any wizards. If an itinerant wizard comes around, she promises to send him out to us. I'm breaking my promise to Ersi, but if the boy is a wizard, there is no need for him to hide.

Elika went on to tell me about a wizard who used to live in the village, but he died a short time before I came. He wasn't terribly old, but she thought he seemed broken down by a hard life. He said he had moved to the Dry Side for the climate. He lived out his life in Deep River but found no suitable apprentice. He left his books to the village — as if they would be of any use! Then she told me his name: Lok! I can only imagine the books he might have collected. I did not tell her I knew him, and I can't say I'm sorry he's gone. Maybe he told the truth about his reason for moving to the Dry Side, but I suspect he was still running from his punishment. Who would look for him in such a remote village? It sounds like he succeeded in punishing himself.

It came as a mild shock to learn whose books Crane had studied. Had he known? Even if Soorhi never told him, Jelf would have known Lok's name as well as Elika did, though it wouldn't have meant as much to either of them as it did to Soorhi. Or now to Elic. The idea of such a person in Deep River gave him a chill, though Lok's reputation paled when compared to that of Yrae. Whose hand Elic had grasped this very night. What a strange world it was.

The next entry was dated almost two months later, in the spring of that year. The writing was more smudged than usual, as if rain had dropped on it. Or tears.

I saw a figure walking toward the swamp. All I could see was a moving blur, but I could tell it was someone walking, not on horseback, so I knew it wasn't Elika. I went to meet him and sensed his power. She had sent us a wizard, and not just any wizard — it was my little Ordy! Wizard Ordahn now, of course, and not little or even all that young. What a joy to hear his voice again! I called Crane in from the vegetable patch. Ordahn asked him the same questions and taught him the same spells Dillum taught Ordy the first time we visited the Wizards' Hall. Crane was delighted. He maste're'd the'm e'asily and de'mande'd more'. Ordahn offe're'd to take' him as his appre'ntice'. I am happy for him. I must be'.

The next entry, dated only a day later, was the one Elic had read when he first found the diary.

My Crane' is gone'. I don't think we' will me'e't again, no matte'r what he' promise's. A gre'at wizard wouldn't come' back to a place' like' this.

When he first read those words, Elic had shared Soorhi's feeling, about a different young wizard. It had seemed as unlikely then that Crane would return to Deep River as that Soorhi's little fellow would come back to the swamp. Elic wasn't sure he believed that now. True, Deep River wasn't a large, important city. But it could be beautiful and pleasant and friendly, a place where even Yrae could know love. It was home.

After a few hours' sleep, Elic rose early to check the weather and the woodpile. A misty drizzle fell, but the morning felt warm enough for the supply of firewood to last through the day, and he expected the woodcutter to deliver more that afternoon. School could resume. As he shouldered through the schoolhouse door with an armload of firewood, he gazed up the road, toward the inn. A large bird flew low, flapping above the roof. An eagle.

"Thank you again, whatever you call yourself," he murmured, and went inside the school.

His students in both classes were a sleepy lot and he couldn't get much work out of them. Even those who hadn't gone to the dance had waited up for family members. Elic put aside his planned lessons and let them talk about the adventure. Some were struck by the journey to Bitter Springs and all the strangers, while others had strong impressions of the dance itself. Elic listened, half awake.

"Teacher, I wanted to dance with you again, but you'd already left," Brynnit said.

"I'm sorry," he replied, shaking himself alert. "I needed my sleep."

"You don't look like you got it," Ylani pointed out.

He chuckled. "You're right about that. I'll have to go to bed early tonight." From the yawns and laughter that greeted this statement, he guessed he wasn't the only one.

As soon as school ended, Elic came fully awake for the first time all day. He hurried to Sunnea's house, the silver pin in his pocket. He half regretted not giving it to her the night before — it would have looked pretty on her best dress — but it was probably just as well. He couldn't have known how warmly they would reconcile. He could hardly wait to see her and present his gift before the magic of the previous night wore off. Halfway there, it occurred to him maybe he should have left the betrothal ring on the shelf until he had her answer. He paused to remove it again, tucking it into his pocket with the pin.

Sunnea answered his knock with a row of pins stuck in the sleeve of her plain, everyday dress — clearly, she'd been helping her father. Her eyes lit up when she saw him, and she looked as lovely as she had in her best dress.

"Elic! Come in." She threw her arms around him. She smelled like roses, but the pins pricked the back of his neck.

"Ow!" he protested.

"Oh! Sorry, let me get rid of these." She pulled the pins out of her sleeve, dropping half of them in her hurry to stick them in the pincushion. When she bent to pick them up, Yshna stopped her.

"I'll get those. Go entertain your caller."

Sunnea guided Elic to the fireside. She offered a chair, but he was too jittery to sit. They stood side by side with their backs to the fire. He turned slightly to look at her profile. A small gold ring glinted from her left ear. He flicked it gently. "So?"

"I put it back last night."

"Me, too." He chuckled at himself. "It felt ... right again. Then on the way here, I took it back out because it also seemed presumptuous."

Sunnea laughed and slapped his shoulder. "You're learning! Do you have it? I'll put it back in for you."

He turned so she had a clear view of his ear. It tickled when she stuck the earring back into the hole and fastened it, but he managed to hold still.

"There, easy as threading a needle," she said.

"Thank you. Do you want to get married?"

"I want to make a life with you."

"Is that a yes?" he asked.

"I would marry you tonight," she whispered.

Elic chuckled. "But your father is making you a

beautiful new dress, and I want to get the house ready. Besides, Pap is making us a cookstove. Spring will be soon enough."

"I suppose you're right. It just seems so far off!"

"We'll have to keep busy getting to know each other again." He slipped his arm around her waist.

"I hope we can always be the way we were last night."

He pulled her close and kissed her. "You mean, like that?"

She giggled. "That, too. I meant what Stell said, that we're a good team. So many couples are in opposition." She glanced past him at her father. "They don't really know each other. I want to know what you think, how you feel, and be on the same side. I want you to know me, the real me, not just the proper, compliant little girl. No secrets."

He kissed her again. "I want that, too." He recalled his promise to Stell. *Well, maybe just one secret. Since it isn't really mine.*

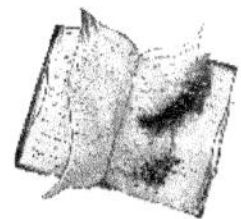

Elic couldn't bring himself to leave Sunnea's side. Every time he started to put on his coat, he remembered something else he needed to tell her or ask her. In the end, he gave up and they pulled their chairs close together in front of the fire. Three silver apple blossoms adorned Sunnea's dress, sapphires glittering in the firelight. Elic and Sunnea held hands and talked about the future while Yshna worked, silent and smiling, across the room.

"I'm planning on putting in a wall to create a second

room across the back," Elic said, sipping from his mug of tea. "Or maybe two small rooms. And later on, we could build an addition. There's already a door there, on the side by the apple tree. What do you think?" He'd made these plans on the day the curse was lifted and had never sought anyone else's opinion about his house. But by spring, it would be *their* house. It was only right that Sunnea have her say in it. She was sure to notice something important he had missed.

Ati emerged from the kitchen and blinked at Elic in apparent, possibly faked, surprise. "This scene looks familiar. Elic, will you stay for supper?" She almost smiled, or at least, her prickles were softer than in recent days.

"Yes, thank you," Elic replied with genuine enthusiasm. He couldn't stop smiling.

"It's nothing fancy, you understand. Just a family supper."

"I couldn't ask for better." He squeezed Sunnea's hand.

They went to the kitchen and sat around the table there. Elic took little notice of the food, but it was a much friendlier meal than the failed betrothal supper.

"What did you two think of the dance?" Elic asked.

"Wasn't that a good time?" Yshna said. "There should be more of them — give the young people a chance to mix, and us old ones a chance to remember what it's like to be young."

Ati pursed her lips, but her expression softened as her gaze fell on Sunnea. "It wasn't so bad. I'm not convinced we should permit such a thing in Deep River."

Sunnea squeezed Elic's hand under the table and hid

a grin. He would have been happy to stay at that table all night, but he had promised himself a full night's sleep. "I should go. Thank you, Ati and Yshna, for your hospitality. Sunnea — thank you." He kissed her in front of everyone, and floated home.

Once there, he felt too elated to sleep. He made himself a cup of tea to help him relax and opened Soorhi's diary. The Crane had left Soorhi in late spring, and the next entry was dated in fall. It began in a now-familiar fashion.

I've had a vision. I saw the village of Deep River, clearer than I ever saw it in life. Elika says they are mostly illiterate there, but in my vision, I knew that someday, someone in Deep River would need to know how to read. I wish I knew who, when, and why. Rather than waste time trying to find out, I'm going to start a school and see what happens. I talked it over with Elika when she came. She's had some education, and wants it for her little girl, so that's one vote in favor. She assures me the folks who keep the inn would feel the same way. She knows the right people to get it started, and she even has a house for me. So this is my new life.

Elic smiled at that. Finally, he had come to the "new life" he regarded as Soorhi's real life. Before reading the diary, he hadn't realized Soorhi's dream of starting a school in Deep River had been a literal vision, but now it made perfect sense. The idea that someday, someone would need to know how to read wasn't idle speculation. But who was that person?

There weren't many entries after that. The handwriting was harder than ever to make out, a sign of Soorhi's steadily worsening eyesight. According to the diary, Elika knew about Soorhi's blindness, but no one else in Deep River ever found out. Elic still found it hard to believe, and he'd read the whole story — almost. He was in the last pages now.

> *Stell's little boy started school today. Can that be? It seems like only yesterday she joined my class. I'm curious about his name, but I can't bring myself to ask. There's some secret there. His voice sounds familiar, and there's something else about him.*

So Soorhi did suspect. Elic doubted he had ever said anything to Crane, who had wondered about his father's identity all his life. There had been no secret Crane was Soorhi's favorite student. The next entry, another Elic had read before, also concerned Crane.

> *Stell's boy has finally revealed his gift. I wish he could have chosen a less dramatic way. It's a good thing I have eyes in the back of my head, as Ordy used to say. As soon as I had my back turned, all the boys crowded around Crane. I saw his hand in*

> *flame's. I didn't think — I move'd: ove'r my de'sk
> and to his side', whe're' I put out the' flame's with
> my hands. I don't know why I wasn't burne'd —
> he' is badly injure'd. He' has le'arne'd a hard le'sson,
> but now he' knows what he' is. It strike's me' again
> that Ste'll name'd him what she' did. He' re'minds me'
> so much of my poor little' fellow. I wish I could
> se'e' his face'.*

The mysteries in this fragment had been solved. Elic knew who everyone was — Ordy, the little fellow, and more than anyone, Soorhi himself. And the *someone* who needed to know how to read must have been Crane. Because he could read, he could understand the spell book, which allowed him to perform the fire spell, thus revealing his power. Once his power was known, he was allowed to study the spell books, training his power enough to free Deep River from Yrae's Curse. In spite of Crane's claim that he had done nothing, Elic believed he had done everything necessary.

A new thought hit Elic like a punch. He'd been questioning the value of education to these children, but he had assumed things would go on as always. He couldn't see the future, after all. But Soorhi could. His vision was about an individual learning to read for some specific purpose. If Soorhi's vision had been fulfilled, was a school in Deep River still needed? If not, Elic wasn't sure what to do. He had no skill at another trade. Even if he learned something else, it wouldn't be the same. Perhaps another school, in another town ... but what about Sunnea? He couldn't lose her again. Would she leave Deep River if he asked her to? It was too much to think about.

He turned the page to the final entry in the book, dated a few days before Soorhi's death.

I hope this is a blank page. I haven't written anything in a long time, but I'm sure I left a few pages empty. I have been too ill to teach the past few days. Young Elic has taken my place, and I hear good things about him. He has a real gift for this work. He's a good teacher, but I suspect there is more in his future than just that. Maybe he's the one I came for, when I had my vision so long ago. The school will be in good hands when I'm gone. The school, and the town. I go in peace.

Elic's low spirits instantly rebounded. He closed the diary and laid it on the table, warmed by those last words of praise from his mentor. And he felt peaceful, too, for the first time in weeks. Maybe Soorhi's vision had been fulfilled in Elic, but Elic's purpose was far from ended. Things were changing and he couldn't see the future, but wasn't that the point? With Sunnea by his side, he could find his new life every day, right here in Deep River. The adventure was only beginning.

The End

About the Author

Karen Eisenbrey lives in Seattle, WA, where she leads a quiet, orderly life and invents stories to make up for it. Karen writes fantasy and science fiction novels, as well as short fiction and the occasional poem or song if it insists. She shares her life with her husband, two young adult sons, and four feline ghosts. Find more info on Karen's books and short fiction, follow her band-name blog, and sign up for her quarterly newsletter at kareneisenbreywriter.com

Special Thanks

... to Ben Gorman for starting a publishing company that
   so perfectly fits my writing; and to M. K. Martin for
   her astute editing.

... to the whole Not A Pipe family of authors for their
   support, encouragement, and example.

... to Michaela for the gorgeous cover art.

... to Angelika, Keith, Maureen, Nan, Steve, Tabitha, and
   Yvonne, my invaluable beta readers.

... to Keith (again), my example for doing the creative
   work that needs to be done in spite of everything else.
   He has read countless drafts (of this and other
   projects), listened to me fuss over ideas, and
   welcomed the host of fictional people who live in my
   head. I couldn't do any of it without him.